nancy rue

'NAMA BEACH HIGH

totally unfair

D1057148

www.youthspecialties.com

www.invertbooks.com

GRAND RAPIDS, MICHIGAN 49530 USA

'Nama Beach High Book 4: Totally Unfair
Copyright ©2005 by Youth Specialties

Youth Specialties Products, 300 South Pierce Street, El Cajon, CA 92020 are published by Zondervan, 5300 Patterson Avenue Southeast, Grand Rapids, MI 49530.

Library of Congress Cataloging-in-Publication Data

Rue, Nancy N.
  Totally unfair / by Nancy Rue.
    p. cm. -- ('Nama Beach High ; bk. 4)
  Summary: Sixteen-year-old Laura Duffy relies on her faith in God when
a vindictive classmate's dishonest tactics turn Laura's best friends
against her.
  ISBN 0-310-25183-4 (pbk.)
  [1. Christian life--Fiction. 2. High schools--Fiction. 3.
Schools--Fiction. 4. Teacher-student relationships--Fiction. 5.
Competition (Psychology)--Fiction.] I. Title.
  PZ7.R88515To 2005
  [Fic]--dc22

2004016917

Web site addresses listed in this book were current at the time of publication. Please contact Youth Specialties via e-mail (YS@YouthSpecialties.com) to report URLs that are no longer operational and replacement URLs if available.

Editorial direction by Laura Gross
Edited by Janie Wilkerson
Proofread by Joanne Heim and Kristi Robison
Cover design by Proxy Design
Interior design by David Conn
Printed in the United States

04 05 06 07 08 09 / DC / 10 9 8 7 6 5 4 3 2 1

chapterone

I was feeling good about my sweet self.

My BFFs or "Best Friends Forever"—according to my sister Bonnie who was six and knew all—were looking at me like I'd just led them to Olympic gold or something.

Okay, I admit—I pretty much felt that way too. Because there they were—Celeste, Stevie, Joy Beth, and Trent—all with bags the size of carry-on luggage under their eyes and hair that hadn't been washed in two days. Who shampoos at a retreat?

But their eyes were shining and their expressions were noble, almost responsible—not something I saw in any of our 16-year-old faces that often.

"Can you believe every single person made the pledge?" I said.

"Yeah, baby, yeah, baby, yeah, baby—yeah!"

That, of course, came from Celeste, who had been straight-faced and principled as long as the rest of the youth group was there. But the minute they went off to pack for home, the freckles across her constantly sunburned face started dancing, and that real-to-the-marrow smile stretched from one dangly rhinestone earring to the other. Only Celeste would wear faux diamonds with a backward ball cap and plaid boxers. And only Celeste could get away with it. She flipped that blond ponytail the way she did everything else—with total comfort inside her own skin.

Stevie, my other best girlfriend, just sat there and smiled. I knew she was recovering from all the high fives and hugs she'd received from the guys in the group before they'd dragged themselves away. Her luscious tousle of highlighted tresses and her deep brown eyes—as well as absolutely everything else about her petite, Latina-flavored self—were impossible for guys to resist. Me, on the other hand, they had no problem resisting.

"Duffy," Celeste said to me. "Read it out loud."

Trent raised his chin from the top of Joy Beth's head where he'd been resting it and scrunched up his very-small-for-a-big-guy mouth. "She's already read it three times."

"No stinkin' way!" Celeste said. Her Brooklyn accent was fully operational. "Where was I?"

Joy Beth grunted. That was her answer to just about everything. Her swimmer's shoulders and her gray-eyed laser gaze created a presence that said it all.

"You were either in the kitchen scavenging," Stevie said, "or changing the spark plugs on Pastor Ennis's car."

"Did I hear my name?" said Pastor Ennis as he passed through with a package of trash bags. "She jumped my battery." He turned his head, shiny to the receding hairline, toward Celeste and added, "Do you change spark plugs?"

"I can be your full-service mechanic, Pastor," Celeste said. She whipped her face toward me, her freckles still doing the cha-cha. "Just read it again, Duffy. I want to hear how awesome it sounds one more time."

It really was a big deal. Our youth group had only been in existence for a couple of months. And although we'd gone from eight members to fifteen in that time, we were still tiny compared to the megachurches in Panama Beach. But there was nothing small about our voices—as we'd shown through our rowdy-'til-dawn pillow fights two nights in a row and, better yet, by the pledge.

"Do it, Duff," Celeste said.

I turned to the giant sticky note on which Stevie had written the pledge. She was a former cheerleader. Cheerleaders could make posters in their sleep.

"Okay," I said. "Here's what we've pledged to do," and I read it to them one more time.

I will be part of the solution for ending hatred in my generation.

I will not harbor any kind of suspicion about people just because they are different from me. I will not tear them down.

I will speak up when other people are showing their ignorance.

I will be sensitive to the hearts of others—even those who seem to have no hearts at all.

I will be strong in my mission to set an example of a caring person and never let my lack of understanding hurt another human being.

I know I can't do this alone. I will continually ask God for his strength and wisdom, empowering my whole generation to stop the hatred.

I will pray for those who hate—for only then can I truly be like God's Son.

Stevie grinned at the BFFs. "And all God's people said—"

"Amen!"

It was a pretty impressive response. And it should have been. I was hoarse from doing it about 20 times over the weekend; we'd amened everything from tacos to "Let's hit the beach." That and all the singing—which I loved—had practically given me laryngitis.

"You really think everybody's going to stick to it?" Trent said.

"You obviously don't," Stevie said.

Joy Beth gave Trent a "love punch" on the arm. "He will."

"I'm not talking about me," Trent insisted. "I'm talking about some of the other guys. They're saying they don't want to preach in the locker room—you know, make fools of themselves."

"Who said they had to make fools of themselves?" I said. "Do they think I'm gonna do that?"

"You did get your jaw broken, Duffy," Celeste said. "And your car stolen—"

"They just don't want to hand out pamphlets or pray in the lunch line," Trent said.

"Hello!" Celeste said. "Who said we were going to do that?"

"I think it's a valid concern." Stevie was also in student government, which meant she had experience with these kinds of heated discussions. "But they don't have to do any of that. And how would we know if they did or didn't anyway? They don't even go to our school."

That was true—they all attended Cove Christian School, a private academy.

"The pledge just says we're going to try to be more decent than most people," Stevie said.

"We can help them with that," Celeste said.

"Absolutely," Stevie said.

YOU two can help them, I thought.

I was glad to have Celeste and Stevie around at times like this. I was Duffy the Responsible One, the Leader, the Girl Who Could Always Get You out of Trouble Because She Was So Good. But I didn't have a gift for stopping male coronary function with a toss of my hair.

Let me just clarify that I wasn't drop-dead ugly or anything. I had sort-of brown, sort-of red hair that was thick, shoulder length, and didn't frizz too much (except when the Florida humidity got higher than the temperature). I wore contacts, so my brown eyes weren't hidden behind glasses, and people said I had a nice smile—although it was shiny with braces. Actually, those metal wires and brackets were going to be things of the past come Monday.

I'd had a couple of boyfriends since I moved to Panama Beach last fall—Richard and Owen—but I was sure they hadn't been with me because of my looks. My looks hadn't *held* them, either. In spite of Celeste's insistence that she was going to get me a date to the junior/senior prom, I'd pretty much sworn off boys at this point in my life.

Pastor Ennis poked his head back into the meeting room. "All right, folks," he said. "Let's get your stuff—we need to get going."

He clapped his hands together the way he did a lot, furry arms glistening. The man had more hair on his forearms and legs than he did on top of his head. He wasn't a geek, though, which was what we'd thought a few months before. He had definitely improved since our first couple of meetings when he used to sweat gallons every time he had to stand up in front of us. But he still did a lot of that hand-clasping thing, like he was sure we were going to pull some evil adolescent caper and reduce him to pastoral tears. Don't think some of the guys hadn't thought of it.

When he ducked out, the BFFs still hung back.

"Did we do good, Duffy?" Celeste said.

"Ya did," I said.

"YOU are responsible for it all, though, Laura," Stevie said. She ran a latte-colored hand down my arm. "I want to be like you when I grow up."

"Stop!" I said.

"Aw, you know you love it," Celeste said.

She threw her arms around my neck for a minisecond and then herded Joy Beth and Trent down the hall. Stevie lingered for her own hug.

"I really am proud to know you, Duffy," she said. "You saved me—you know that. If I were still hanging around with Gigi Palmer and her crowd, I would be on probation just like they are—or worse."

"You never would have stooped to their level," I said. After all the trouble Gigi Palmer had caused me, I knew her level was about six feet below everybody else's. "But you ARE out of that group now, and it's partly because of you that they aren't going to give us any more grief."

"No, it's SO you, Duff. You are one of the best people I've ever known."

The look she gave me added two inches to my five-foot-seven frame. In another minute she'd have me walking on water.

We settled into our seats in the church's revamped school bus and sang the whole hour-and-a-half it took us to drive back to Panama Beach. One thing I loved to do was belt it out, and I was getting into it even more since I'd gotten my jaw unwired. I'd moved to Panama Beach eight months before, but I hadn't gotten to sing much because I'd arrived two weeks into the school year and couldn't get into Mr. Howitch's to-die-for music program. I had managed to land a part in the fall musical, but then the jaw thing happened. I eventually wanted to pursue a career as a singer—and now I had to make up for lost time. I mean, good grief, I was already a junior.

I was so hoarse from all the singing and yelling and shrieking we'd been doing all weekend, I sounded more like an alto than my usual soprano at that point. But by the time I got home and joined my parents and Bonnie at the dinner table, I sounded like a baritone.

"What else did you leave at the retreat—besides your voice?" my dad said. The skin around his eyes was crinkling. He never exactly smiled—he just crinkled.

Mom put a plate piled with salad, green beans, and some kind of corn thing in front of me. "I bet you lived on Cheetos and Dr Pepper the whole weekend," she said.

Her fading blondish hair was a mass of curls—just like Bonnie's—and they quivered as she bobbed her head at me. "I don't even have to ask if you had a good time," she said. "You're glowing." Her blue eyes—also like Bonnie's—grew rounder. "But you look tired. I want you in bed early tonight. Both of you."

"Not me!"

That protest came from my little sister, who until then had been concentrating on eating *around* the green beans. She was glaring indignantly at Mom, her little bow of a mouth pursed. Bonnie was like a little Mom, and I was a female version of Dad. It was amazing how the genes got divided up and handed out.

"I wasn't talking about you," Mom said to her. "I meant Laura and your daddy."

Dad cocked an eyebrow.

"Was he bad?" Bonnie said.

"No—but he's starting back to work full time tomorrow, and he needs a good night's sleep."

"Thank you, Mommy," Dad said.

The crinkles around his eyes AND mouth were in motion. We were used to my mother protectively clucking around all of us, and that included my dad—especially since his recent accident. She was a total mom to the core—right down to how she placed the folded socks in neat rows in our drawers and decorated the kitchen in green checks and apples.

"I have to go along on Bonnie's field trip tomorrow—" she was saying now.

"Tallahassee—yay!" Bonnie said.

"So you're going to have to go to the orthodontist on your own, Laura. Are you all right with that?"

"It's all good, Mom," I said, voice croaking. "I need to go finish my homework."

"And then lights out."

I tried not to roll my eyes at her. My parents and I had come a long way since we'd moved to Florida from Missouri back in September—back when I held them responsible for all of my misery. But they still watched me pretty closely, like I'd just learned to walk and they were now afraid I'd run into a wall or wander out into the street. I really couldn't blame them. I had a way of getting myself into "situations"—right up to my eyeballs.

Dad was now eyeing me, and I couldn't help but notice his thinner-than-usual face. He'd lost a lot of weight since his injury.

"You aren't trying to do too much again, are you?" he said to me.

"No, sir," I said.

He watched me for a minute. "You might not be DOING too much, but you're obviously TALKING too much. Let's skip the Cereal Meeting tonight so you can get some rest."

That was kind of a bummer. The Cereal Meeting was a thing Dad and I did after Mom and Bonnie were in bed and my homework was done. We'd meet in the kitchen, eat a couple bowls of oatmeal or some contraband Trix cereal (we kept it hidden because Bonnie was allergic to it—and just about everything else that tasted good to a kid), and just talk. If it weren't for those nightly meetings, my father and I might never have discovered that we were not from different alien galaxies after all.

I kissed my folks, hugged Bonnie and told her I'd read her *two* stories tomorrow night, and retreated down the hall to my room.

I HAD to finish my homework. Unfortunately, tonight's assignment came from MAPPS (the honors program) chemistry, something that made about as much sense to me as Morse code. Trent had tried to convince me to take my textbook to the retreat so he could tutor me during free time. I told him he was nuts and that progress reports were coming out on Monday so it was too late anyway.

When I finally tumbled into bed, I closed my eyes and turned to God. For me, praying had become a running dialogue throughout the day. But having 14 people in my face all weekend long during the retreat, I'd hardly remembered to brush my teeth, much less talk to God—or really listen to him—on my own—you know, apart from the praise and worship we all did together.

As I lay there in the deep stillness of my bedroom, I breathed him in and breathed out the junk. Stuff like how K.J.—another girl in Mrs. Isaacsen's talk group with Stevie, Celeste, Joy Beth, and me—had told me that getting my braces off was going to be like having my teeth ripped out.

Or the fact that if I got less than a B in chemistry, my parents were going to be on me even more about all the stuff I was involved in, including my stage crew job for *The Crucible*. It was opening in two weeks, and tech week was going to mean night rehearsals starting Tuesday. I couldn't let Mr. Howitch down. He was by far the most amazing music and drama teacher ever. Maybe the most incredible teacher, period. Next to Mrs. Isaacsen, of course, who was so much more to me than just a guidance counselor. If it weren't for her, I would still be saying, "Now I lay me down to sleep" and calling it a night.

She was that much a part of my spiritual journey.

I breathed it all out while I breathed in God—Father, Son, and Holy Spirit—until I got to that peaceful place where I could simply be in his presence.

Father, I breathed to him. *Thank you. Thank you for the weekend. The pledge. The feeling of doing something I know is your will, something that's going to help anyone who's suffering from hate.*

I settled in more deeply and felt the warmth of connecting with my Father. It was a true space. A quiet place. A wonder I knew I didn't create.

Thank you for delivering me from the hate of people like Gigi and her friends. Thank you for being.

Please give us a mission to protect even more people from the hatred of others. Use us, Lord. Please use us.

I took one more long breath and drifted off into sleep, where God would be with me like a whisper in my dreams.

chaptertwo

Getting my braces off early the next morning was sort of anticlimactic after the big weekend. All the ripping and wrenching and bloodshed K.J. had so deliciously described to me didn't happen.

Afterward I headed for school and looked at myself in the rearview mirror of my old Mercedes—which Celeste and her father fixed up for me. I decided I didn't look that much different without the metal in my mouth.

Somewhere along the way I guess I had stopped thinking the braces made me look like Geek Girl. For somebody who had to stare at Celeste and Stevie all day, that was a good sign. Still it would be fun to see how I looked singing without my braces. Or it would have been if I didn't sound like Kermit the Frog after the weekend. I let the radio play without me.

When I got my progress report during second-period homeroom, I was lifted up another notch. Except for a B in honors chemistry, I got all A's. During our lunch period out in the courtyard, however, Trent got grumbly.

"What's your deal?" Celeste said to him.

"She could've gotten an A if she'd kept up with the tutoring."

But I was looking at Joy Beth, who had broken her bologna sandwich into pieces and was now pushing them around on top of the plastic bag. When Joy Beth didn't inhale her lunch, something was definitely wrong.

"What's up, Joy Beth?" I said.

She shook her head. Trent mouthed, "SWIM MEET," like it was a big secret. We'd talked about almost nothing else the entire week before. It was Joy Beth's first one since she'd been diagnosed with diabetes last summer. She'd had so much trouble getting her blood sugar under control, for a while it looked like she was going to have to give up her dream of becoming an Olympic swimmer. In fact, if she didn't blow everybody away at the rest of her meets, the dream might just evaporate anyway.

"Nervous?" I said to her.

Trent gave me a "why-are-you-bringing-this-up?" look. Joy Beth grunted twice.

"Did y'all notice that Duffy got her braces off?" Stevie said. "Doesn't she look fabulous?"

I ignored her.

"I'd be nervous, too," I said to Joy Beth.

Trent practically popped his contacts as he glared at me.

"It's okay to admit to your feelings," I said.

"I just want this real bad," Joy Beth said. "And I don't wanna let the team down, neither."

"Are you kidding me?" Trent said. He turned his eyes on Joy Beth as if she'd just been crowned Miss Panama Beach. "You're going to make everybody else look like they're doing the dog paddle."

Joy Beth suddenly ducked her head. If her hair hadn't been trimmed to just below her chin, Coach's orders, two panels of not-quite-blond hair would be covering her face about now. But I could clearly see the blotches of embarrassment on her cheeks.

"Is it okay that I'm scared?" she said.

"Well, yeah," I said. "I mean—you're a human being, for Pete's sake."

She hung her head down farther.

"What?" I said.

By then Celeste and Stevie were tuning back in.

"What's going on?" Celeste said.

"I'm scared spitless—that's what's goin' on!" Joy Beth said.

The two little freshman girls at the next table gave us nervous looks over the tops of their brown bags. Joy Beth could be pretty intimidating when she got wound up.

"Duh," Celeste said. "This meet's humongatory for you. I'm surprised you're not in the bathroom with your head in the toilet."

"But it's wrong!" Joy Beth's face was going purple. I feared for Trent, who was within shoving range should she decide to bolt from the table.

"Why is it wrong, sugar?" Stevie said.

"Because." Joy Beth looked right at me. "Because if you have faith, you aren't supposed to be afraid! Duffy says that all the time!"

I leaned across the table at her. "I never said that! I said God doesn't WANT us to be afraid because he has everything under control. But we're human, so we still get scared—but then we do what we have to do anyway because we know he's really in charge . . ."

I trailed off because it was obvious nothing I said was going to be able to penetrate that mask of defeat on her face.

"She needs prayer," Stevie said.

"Let's do it," Celeste said.

We held hands and then, of course, they all looked to me to start.

"Okay, so God?" I said. "Joy Beth's scared—"

"Spitless," Celeste put in.

"This meet is something she's been getting ready for for months—you already know that—so please, would you give her the strength and the courage to go for it? She feels like this is what you made her for, so please help her to know that you've given her everything she needs. Help Joy Beth have faith in that."

"And all God's people said—"

I waited. We all breathed out an *amen.*

"I love it when you pray, Duffy," Celeste said.

"I'm glad YOU do," said a voice above us, "because the rest of us don't."

I looked up to see Gigi Palmer's practically purple eyes glaring down at me.

I had to force myself not to groan out loud. The question, *Is she starting this AGAIN?*, was immediately at the front of my brain.

But how could she be? After her last attack Gigi had received a huge suspension, hours of community service, and no participation in extracurricular activities for six weeks. Why would she take a chance by harassing us right there in the courtyard when any more trouble would probably land her in juvenile hall?

But she didn't look cautious now. She was slanting her eyes at me like she always did, as if I were breaking some rich kid rule by breathing her air. She slung her dark, blue-black hair over her shoulders and fixed her mouth in a sneer. Actually, no matter what was going on, she always looked like she'd just picked up the scent of something foul.

"I'd move on if I were you, Gigi," Stevie said, using her student government voice.

"But you're not me, are you?" Gigi said. "You don't even come *close* to being me anymore."

"As if she ever did," Celeste muttered.

"Whatever," Stevie said. "You're going to get yourself in trouble if you hang around us."

"I'm going to get in trouble for expressing my feelings?" Gigi said.

"What feelings?" Celeste said.

Instead of answering her, Gigi turned to the girl standing next to her. I hadn't even noticed her until just then. She was shorter than Gigi—her handmaidens usually were—and she had a mop of curly chestnut hair bigger than she was and more freckles than Celeste. I was surprised Gigi hadn't ordered her to have them bleached out.

"What did I tell you?" Gigi said to the girl. "They're the ones who turn everything into a battle, and then I get in trouble for it."

I opened my mouth to SO deny that, and then I closed it. What was the point? Gigi was beyond reason.

She bent over me, hair sliding, her sneer still fixed. "I'm not going to get in trouble for informing you that praying in public is offensive to some of us."

"And your very existence is offensive to some of US," Celeste said.

I kicked her under the table. Tact wasn't one of her many skills.

"But there's no LAW against ME," Gigi said. "And there IS a law against pushing your religion in a public school."

She looked smugly at the chick beside her.

"Are you done?" Stevie said.

Gigi tossed her hair back as she straightened up and twisted her mouth. "For now."

Then she gave her handmaiden a nod, and they strode through the courtyard like they were parting the waters. I secretly hoped they would both drown.

"Is that true? Is it against the law to pray in school?" Joy Beth said.

"No stinkin' way!" Celeste said. "What would Gigi know about it?"

"Who was that girl with her?" Trent always liked to know who the enemy was.

"Her name's Fielding Hall," Stevie said. "She's new—she's in my art class."

"Art?" Celeste said. "You get paint on your manicure in art. Gigi'll have her out of there in no time."

"What I wanna know," Joy Beth said, "is if that prayer WAS against the law, does it still count?"

"Of course it does!" I said. "Since when did God follow OUR laws?"

"That's good," Joy Beth said, "because I think it's workin'." She took in a huge breath, impressively filling up her sizable chest. "I'm gonna kick some serious tail in that swim meet."

We said *amen* without any reminder this time. I wondered if Gigi heard it. I decided I hoped so.

✳ ✳ ✳

The whole scene faded into the background by the time we all met at the pool that afternoon. I raced out of *Crucible* rehearsal and tore all the way across campus to make it by 4 p.m., and I was breathing like a steam shovel when I got there. K.J. was right on my heels the entire way.

K.J. was the youngest one in Mrs. Isaacsen's Group. Although she hung out with me and the BFFs sometimes—seeing as how we'd seen her through some really rotten stuff not long before—she put most of her 14-year-old energy into theater. She played the part of Mary Warren in *The Crucible*.

At one time K.J. had run with the "I've smoked so much weed I'm in a stupor crowd." Now she avoided them like they had leprosy. Not only would Mr. Howitch boot her right out of the production if she got into any trouble, but she was also living with Mrs. Isaacsen because she'd refused to stay with her abusive father when her parents divorced. Meanwhile, her mother was in an alcohol rehabilitation facility and would have to prove she was a fit mother when she got out. Whenever I thought I had big problems, I thought about K.J. and felt like a wimp.

"Where's everybody sitting?" I tried to shout to K.J. She was way ahead of me by this time. The girl ran like a deer—even in her current outfit, which featured a tight skirt slithering down from her hips. K.J. always pushed the envelope with her apparel. Mrs. I. obviously hadn't checked her over before she left for school that morning.

K.J. flipped her head back toward me, her silky, honey-brown hair slipping across her face. "Hey—" she said, "You DID get your braces off."

"Yeah, it feels weird—"

"Sounds weird, too. What's wrong with your voice?"

"I—"

"We're sitting with Mrs. I.—second set of bleachers." She rolled her almond-colored eyes that matched her hair. "I feel like I'm on a leash."

But I knew she didn't mind it that much. I would have LOVED to live with Mrs. Isaacsen. My parents were cool, but they didn't talk about their journey with God the way Mrs. I. did.

When we got inside the gate to the pool, a throng of kids was just standing there, deciding whether to stay for the meet or to keep their options open. Heaven forbid they should commit to something. I stood on tiptoes and spotted Mrs. I.'s head of crisp, short, salt-and-pepper hair. She was observing the crowd from behind her sunglasses, which didn't surprise me because she loved teenagers like nobody else I had ever known. I sometimes told her she was a sick woman.

What did jar me a little was the fact that she wasn't smiling. Mrs. I. always had at least a wry twitch going on. She was one of those people who loved life and lived it abundantly. Right then she looked the way most OTHER teachers looked at school sporting events—like they're on duty at the state pen. That wasn't like our Mrs. I.

"There's Celeste," K.J. said.

It was hard to miss her. Celeste, wearing a sizzling pink minidress with matching sandals, was standing on the bleachers and waving her arms. She was in '70s mode; Celeste had a different look every day.

By the time we climbed over about 30 people to get to the seats Celeste, Stevie, and Trent were saving for us, the meet was about to start. Trent was gnawing at his fingernails and blinking his eyes against his contacts as if they were filled with sand. He did that when he got nervous. I hoped Joy Beth wasn't as stressed out as he was.

I squeezed in between Mrs. I. and Celeste before allowing my eyes to search the pool area for Joy Beth. She was standing a little apart from the rest of the team, and she looked so well-toned in her aqua and orange tank suit—the 'Nama Beach colors—that I looked at Trent to see if he'd noticed. If he did, it was making him bite his cuticles.

"She looks great!" I said.

"Yes, she does," Mrs. I. said. "And so do you." She tapped her teeth with her fingernail and gave me an absent smile.

My heart took a little dip. There was definitely something funky about her. Normally she would have hugged my neck and whipped out some kind of getting-your-braces-off celebration present—AND handed me a choice of throat lozenges for my voice.

"You okay?" I said to her.

"Hmm?"

Celeste poked me from the other side. "Check out the dude with the hairy chest. Is he not marvelicious in those swim trunks?"

"Marvelicious?" I said. Lately, Celeste had picked up the habit of combining parts of words to make up her own.

"You know you think he's gorgeous."

"He's okay."

"He's a total babe—and I happen to know he doesn't have a prom date yet."

I tried to turn back to Mrs. Isaacsen, but Celeste was like a bulldog.

"I can set up a meeting for you," she said.

"No!" I said. The higher my pitch went, the less voice I had.

Celeste pulled a pink visor out of her backpack and stuck it on her head. "I will wear you down, Duffy."

I sighed.

"I'm introducing you to Mr. Hairy Chest," she said. "You're more splendicious than ever without the braces."

But then we were both pulled to attention when six swimmers took their places at the end of the pool. The voice on the intercom squealed out that it was time for the 400-meter freestyle.

Joy Beth was among them, looking focused and stern and powerful on the starting block—her eyes straight ahead as she shook her arms out to the sides and got ready to throw herself forward.

"I imagine the whole race in my head before I start," she'd told me once. "It's kinda like prayin'."

Celeste and Stevie both stood up and yelled, "You go, Joy Beth! Go, girl!" as if she could actually hear them. I stayed next to Mrs. I., who squeezed my hand.

When the starting gun went off, Joy Beth skimmed out onto the water. It was hard to make out her big, beefy arms; they were digging in and out of the water that fast.

"Come ON, Joy Beth!" Celeste screamed.

She was neck and neck with two other swimmers; the three leaders left the rest of their opponents midpool. For what seemed like a semester, the trio cut through the pool as one. But then Joy Beth began to dig harder and faster until she was like a well-oiled, fine-tuned machine.

Suddenly, there was space between her and the others, as if she'd made the jump to hyperspace. Nobody could catch her—and Joy Beth's hand touched the side of the pool a whole second before the swimmer from Lynn Haven High.

She surfaced to a unanimous cheer from the stands, turning her face the color of salsa. And then she grinned and waved at the crowd, like a champion acknowledging her adoring fans. I stood up then—all the way up on the bench—and yelled stuff that never made it past my tonsils. She looked up at us, and her grin got bigger.

"She's got the relay after this next race," Trent said. He was still chowing down on his nails.

Celeste tugged at my sleeve. "Mr. Hairy Chest is going to swim now. Look at the pecs on this guy."

I could feel my stomach going into a knot. I really, REALLY didn't want to get involved with another male. Richard had been a heartbreak that had taken forever to heal; and when I'd finally trusted Owen, he'd dropped out of sight the minute I got involved in something that scared him.

There just isn't any boy I want to invest my time in, I thought.

Except one—and I wasn't even sure who he was. I might never see him again. I hadn't heard from him in weeks.

I stuffed him back into the off-limits place in my mind and pretended to cheer as the swimmers splashed their way into the second lap. I was feeling uneasy all of a sudden, and that feeling wasn't going to be lifted by some dude in a Speedo.

If only I could convince Celeste of that.

chapter three

After the meet the BFFs and I headed for a sub shop to celebrate with Joy Beth. She'd won her individual event AND saved the team in the relay. It was my last free evening before I had to start tech rehearsals, too. I was going to miss hanging out with them the way I did most of the time.

We took our sandwiches outside where there were a couple of tables we could pull together. Celeste stood up on one of the plastic chairs, raised her soda, and said, "To Joy Beth—Olympic gold!"

We clacked cups, and I ended up wearing some of Trent's Coke on the sleeve of my white shirt.

"You couldn't have ordered a Sprite?" I said to him.

He looked wounded.

"It's okay," I said. "I'll go in the bathroom and get it off."

"Wait—not before we toast Stevie," Celeste said. She was still on the chair, waving her drink around. I needed to get out of there before she washed my hair with it.

"Me?" Stevie said. "What did I do?"

"It's what you're gonna do," Celeste said. "Hello—you're running for student body president!"

I stopped halfway out of my seat. "You decided, Stevie?"

She nodded. "I'm going to do it. I want to make student government something besides a party club. S.G. can make a difference, y'all, and I want to be the one to make that happen."

"To the next student body president of Panama Beach High!" Celeste said.

I barely escaped getting a carbonated shampoo and scooted to the bathroom. I was unsuccessfully scrubbing at my sleeve with a brown paper towel when Celeste appeared and perched herself on the edge of the sink.

"All right, Duffy," she said. "We have to have a serious talk about the prom."

I rolled my eyes at my reflection in the mirror. "Celeste, would you give it UP? I don't care about going out with some guy. I really don't."

"So don't go with a guy. Go with Stevie and me. Trent's taking Joy Beth—no-brainer—so the three of us can go together. It'll be the bomb!"

"You both have dates."

"No, we've both been asked. Neither one of us has accepted yet."

I tossed the paper towel into the trash can and looked at her. "Neither one of you has decided WHICH invitation to accept yet. There is no way I'm going to let you give up the whole fairy-tale prom thing because you feel sorry for me."

"Get outta town!" she said. "This isn't a pity party. Why would we want to spend an evening trying to keep some boy out of our prom dresses if we can hang out with you instead?"

I shook my head. "Nice try—and I appreciate it; I really do. But WHY are you so determined to make me do this?"

Celeste folded her arms and looked at the ceiling.

"WHAT?" I said.

"I just think you're so serious about everything all the time—and I'm not saying that isn't good—but I want to see you have some fun once in a while. Cut loose."

"I'll have a cookie with my turkey sub," I said. "How's that?"

She wrinkled her freckles and went ahead of me out of the bathroom. I followed at a deliberately slower pace. My mind was going to that off-limits place again.

There's really only one guy I'm interested in, I thought. Every time I considered dating some other guy—like THAT was gonna happen—I got this picture of Ponytail Boy in my head.

That was what I called him because I didn't know his name. The few times I—or anybody else—had seen him, he'd had his long, sun-touched brown hair tied back at the nape of his neck. But what really haunted me were his eyes, brown but somehow gold, bright yet soft enough to go deep. He had something I couldn't fathom, something that drew me to him even though he was in and out of my life like a wisp of smoke.

And it's always when I'm in a crisis, I thought. *I don't think the prom qualifies.*

Besides, now that I was so connected with God, there weren't going to be any more traumatic events in my life. Which was probably why, I realized, there had been no recent Ponytail Boy sightings and no more gifts or parchment paper notes left in my locker by my Secret Admirer—who I was sure was Ponytail Boy himself. At least, as certain as I could be when it came to him.

"Duffy!"

Celeste was holding the front door open and popping her eyes at me.

"What?" I said.

"I've only said your name like 18 times. Smile—I'm about to introduce you to somebody."

Before I could even try to make an escape back toward the bathroom, she grabbed a passing guy by the arm and sparkled a smile at him.

"Hey, Duckie!" she said.

Duckie? She had NOT just said that, had she?

I looked—reluctantly—at the boy with light reddish hair who was now hugging Celeste. She knew every boy at 'Nama, I was sure, and had dated most of them until the BFFs formed. She always said that we'd saved her from being transformed into a full-blown idiot by males. I kind of thought the opposite was true—Celeste transformed the guys, seeing how she never really committed to any of them. Thank goodness.

She was now greeting this dude like he was her long-lost fiancé. He was tall and had shoulders like a construction worker. His blue-gray eyes were probably big, though at the moment he seemed to be concentrating on keeping them nonchalantly half-closed. His whole face, in fact, was deliberately serious as he stood there letting Celeste grill him about his immediate love status. Duckie was trying very hard to look like Mr. Bad, but his turned-up nose belied the whole thing. In fact, he reminded me so much of a little boy, I clamped my hand over my mouth to smother a smile. It was obvious he wasn't about to smile.

"Oh—my bad!" Celeste said as she turned to me. "This is my friend Laura Duffy!"

As if she hadn't planned the whole thing.

"Duff, this is Duck. His name's actually Neil Duckwell." Celeste hugged his arm. "Everybody calls him Duck."

"YOU call him Duck," I said.

But "Duck" shook his head and ran his hand over his choppy hair. "No—everybody calls me that. Except Coach Powell. He calls me Slacker."

"You're on the swim team?" I said.

"Thanks for noticing," he said.

"I was too busy focusing on Joy Beth," I said—quickly, so Celeste wouldn't deck me.

Duck nodded solemnly. "She was awesome."

"She's not all about herself, though. I mean—she wanted to score points for the team."

"She's about the only one who thinks about the team," Duck said. He seemed to write the rest of them off with a jerk of his head.

I turned to include Celeste in the conversation, but she was gone. A glance through the front window revealed her sitting back at the table, sneaking a peek at me over her shoulder, her head bent next to Stevie's. I could have throttled them both.

"So—how do you know Celeste?" Duck said.

I stared at him for a few seconds. Why he hadn't taken that opportunity to make a quick getaway, I didn't know. He didn't look stupid—he knew as well as I did that Celeste had set him up. How could you know Celeste for ten minutes without being able to figure that out?

"We're in a group together," I said.

"Singing group?"

I laughed. "Uh, no. Celeste couldn't sing her way out of a plastic bag. It's one of the few things she can't do."

"But you sing. I mean, you do when you don't have laryngitis."

He said it more like a statement than a question.

"I do," I said. "I came to 'Nama too late in the year to get into chorus, but next year it's totally going to be my big thing."

"You'll get a lead role in the musical, I bet."

"You've never even heard me sing," I said.

"Yeah, I have."

"When? I've never performed at 'Nama!"

"I heard you at the hospital back in—whenever it was. You know—when you did that vigil thing for your dad."

"You were there?" I said.

He nodded.

"Why?"

He shrugged. "Why not? I think stuff like that is cool."

I stared again. There was no way to tell if he was for real or not because his expression hadn't changed.

And then it did. He smiled.

It was like someone completely different was standing in front of me. With his teeth gleaming and a faint pair of dimples indenting his cheeks, he looked even younger. It was as if he'd forgotten who he was trying to be.

I figured I owed him for the effort, so I gave him a smile back. "Well, thanks. Next time I'll try to notice you when you're swimming—"

I practically bit my tongue in two. Did that sound like a come-on or what? Duck's smile went back to wherever it had come from, and he gave me a nod. "I guess I'll see you around," he said.

"Sure," I said.

At least I got to be the first one to turn and walk away. Flee is more like it—right out the front door and over to the table where my supposedly best friends were pretending they hadn't just had me under surveillance.

"He liked you!" Celeste whispered so that anyone on the strip mall could have heard her. "I've only known him about a week, but I figured he'd get into your husky new voice. I think you oughta try to keep it—"

"He did NOT like me," I said. "And don't ever do that again."

"You're not seriously upset?" Stevie said.

I sank into a chair in front of my uneaten sandwich. "A little. Celeste—please—no boys, okay? They just mess up my head. I'm totally clear on things right now, and I don't need—I don't want—a guy. Period."

Celeste looked momentarily miserable, and then she brightened. "Okay," she said, ponytail bouncing. "So the three of us will go to prom together."

"No—you two go with your dates—"

"What dates?" Stevie said. "I'm not going to the prom unless you go."

"Me neither," Celeste said.

They looked very proud of themselves, like they had just staged a coup. I should have been grateful, maybe, but I felt like I was in a position I wouldn't have wished on Gigi herself.

I started talking to God about it—seriously—right then. Matter of fact, I was breathing him in like I was having an asthma attack.

chapterfour

Dad went to bed early that night after his first full day back at work. Mom said he was "a whupped puppy." So once I read the obligatory two stories to Bonnie—or actually, SHE read them to ME because she said my voice was too "crackly"—I used what would have been Cereal Meeting time to curl up on my bed. I left the window open so I could catch the honeyed smell of the sweet alyssum Mom had planted in my window box and the grunts of the frogs imitating my voice. I sipped on the hot apricot nectar Mom gave me to help my throat—even though I kept telling her it didn't hurt, which it didn't—and had a major breathing treatment with God.

So, Father, I was feeling so good about everything at the retreat—y'know, when we all agreed to the pledge. And now all this little stuff is crowding in—you know what I'm saying?

Gigi's back at it. I don't really get why you don't just shut people like her up. I mean, really—I'm the one losing my voice here! And this whole boy thing. Why does Celeste keep missing the part where I say I don't WANT to go out with anybody, to the prom or anywhere else?

And what's up with Mrs. I.? She seems way distracted, and it's creeping me out a little bit. Is it just my imagination? I can get carried away sometimes—but, then, you know that.

I pulled in the scent of Mom's garden, all sweet and fragrant and soft just like her. I liked the velvety way it felt to realize—again—that

God knew me better than I knew myself. HE was the one who surprised ME—all the time.

I put my hand up to the light and watched the tiny silver keys on my bracelet dance against my wrist. Mrs. I. had given it to me. Every time I'd learned about another key to the secret power God had for me, she'd added another key charm.

One for surrendering to God as the only one who has control.

Another for giving up everything that I thought was important so I could see what was really significant in his eyes.

And the third for being willing to give up my life for my friends so they could know what God's love really was.

I have everything I need, don't I? my breath whispered.

There wasn't an answer. Sometimes I'd feel a slight tugging, like I was being pulled along by a silken rope. Other times there would be a whisper in my mind. But this time I just felt tired. I nestled in under the sheets and let the frogs croak me to sleep.

Mom offered to keep me home the next morning so my throat could heal, but I was too anxious to get to our Group meeting and maybe have a few minutes alone with Mrs. Isaacsen. Whenever I was struggling with stuff, I always ran it by her. She had some kind of inner sense that never seemed to be wrong.

Michelle was the only person in Mrs. I.'s office when Stevie and I got there. As usual she was sitting primly, her knees crossed in tidy fashion just below the hem of a fitted gray skirt, and writing something in a date book. The first couple of times I'd seen Michelle, all sleek and poised and black, I'd thought she was a student teacher from Florida State. As it turned out, she was only a sophomore at 'Nama Beach. There was just something so mature about her—and something so disdainful in her attitude toward the rest of us. I'd seen her look at Celeste and K.J. and me as if she were supervising a preschool class.

Even though it was like trying to befriend a refrigerator, I always at least made an attempt at conversation with the girl.

"What's up with you these days?" I said.

She looked up from the date book and said flatly, "I have to drop the Group."

"No!" Stevie said. "Why?"

"It's a time thing. I can't be in the Business Club because I don't have time to earn enough points—" She flicked a hand in her hair. "Whatever. I'm going to work here in the guidance office during activity period instead."

Celeste and K.J. arrived then, and Michelle folded back into herself. Celeste's eyes were sparkling behind the little wire-rimmed glasses she wore today. Celeste, of course, had 20/20 vision.

"I saw Duck in the hall just now," she said. "He said he thinks you're hot, Duffy."

"A duck thinks you're hot?" K.J. said to me. Her faint eyebrows went up. "I guess if you're that desperate for a prom date—"

"His NAME is Duck!" Stevie said.

Michelle let out a disgusted puff of air. In the doorway Joy Beth grunted.

"I am NOT desperate for a prom date!" I said. "And I am NOT interested in Duck Boy—so would everyone just back OFF?"

I turned in time to see Mrs. Isaacsen rushing in, several pink phone message slips in her hand. My heart took a definite dive. Her eyes were so distant, I was sure she hadn't even noticed we were in the room yet.

"Are you all right?" Stevie said to her.

"I need for all of you to take out a piece of paper," Mrs. I. said.

A piece of paper? We TALKED in Group—none of us had picked up a pencil in that office since we'd started meeting.

I wasn't the only one who was in shock. Celeste was staring with her mouth open, a Get outta town! frozen on her lips. K.J. and Stevie were exchanging baffled glances, and even Michelle's eyes were uncharacteristically bulging at the moment.

As we shuffled around for paper in our backpacks and dug for pens, the room seemed to frost over. The room with the frog clock and the bright rug. The room where I'd drunk tea and delved into my soul with Mrs. Isaacsen over and over again. The room where I had always, always felt safe.

"I'm sorry if we were too rowdy when you came in," I said.

"You were fine," Mrs. I. said. And then she sighed as if she'd been holding back the last 15 breaths she was supposed to have taken. "I'm sorry, girls. I have a lot on my mind, and I need for you to do something quiet this period while I take care of some things."

"Hey, you want to talk about it?" Celeste said. "You've trained us how to be good listeners."

For an instant a glimmer went through Mrs. Isaacsen's eyes. "You'd have a field day with this, my loves. Thanks, but I need to handle it—and I really need to do it now."

She had us write a response to our last Group meeting—about where we were in our journey toward personal power—or in my case, God power.

I've come so far, Mrs. I., I wrote. *I feel like there's nothing God and I can't handle together. I hope that doesn't sound trite because it's really true.*

The minute the BFFs and I got to our lunch table in the courtyard, of course, I was all over it.

"So WHAT is wrong with Mrs. I.?" I said.

Stevie leaned in. "Do you think it's menopause?"

"What?" Celeste said.

"That's when you stop—" Stevie said.

"I KNOW what it is," Celeste said. "But she's not old enough, is she?"

Joy Beth gave a half grunt. "You heard her say she has a lot on her mind."

"But what is it?" I said. "I mean, whatever it is, it's huge. She doesn't usually go down with stuff."

"I bet I know." Stevie was twirling a strand of hair around a finger.

"What?" I said.

"I bet she's just now realizing she bit off more than she can chew by having K.J. live with her. She's a good kid—but she tries to get away with everything. Did you check out the outfit she has on today?"

I shook my head.

"It's one of those tops that crosses over in the front. Only it didn't quite cross."

"She's barin' it and sharin' it," Celeste said.

I was shaking my head again. "I don't think it's K.J. Mrs. I. wouldn't have talked about it in front of her if it were. And besides, you said Mrs. I. had bitten off more than she could chew. I think she can chew quite a bit. She's Mrs. I.!"

Or at least she used to be. A shadow crossed my mind, as if there were already an empty space where my warm Mrs. I. thoughts used to guide me.

Still, that night at rehearsal while Benjamin, our roly-poly stage manager, was explaining how we were supposed to sign in, I worked my way over to where K.J. was sitting on the floor with her eyes closed.

"Hey," I whispered to her.

She opened one eye and slanted it toward me. "What?" she said.

"I just wondered if you know what's going on with Mrs. I."

K.J. closed her eye again and shrugged.

"Does that mean 'no' or 'I don't know'?" I whispered.

"It means I'm not thinking about that right now."

"Laura," someone whispered behind me.

I turned around to see Deirdre, my chemistry lab partner. She was playing the role of one of the girls of Salem who accused people of being witches. They went nuts and screamed through every scene they were in. Deirdre had been typecast for the role.

"K.J.'s getting into character," she hissed to me. "She does it before every rehearsal. Sometimes she makes weird noises with her nose—"

"Deirdre," K.J. said without opening her eyes.

"Yeah?"

"Shut up."

Deirdre nodded sagely. "She does THAT before every rehearsal, too."

When Deirdre melted away, I still waited another 15 seconds, watching K.J. It was totally OUT of character for her to pass up an opportunity to dig out somebody's private information. When she didn't at least say she'd see what she could find out about Mrs. I. and report back to me, I reluctantly returned to my place backstage.

The rest of the stage crew gathered, and Benjamin joined us, his face beaming red even in the darkness of the wings. His T-shirt was already damp, and we hadn't even started yet. The boy could break a sweat just crossing the room with his script.

"This is our first complete run-through before we start adding costumes—lights—makeup—"

This I already knew. Unlike the rest of the stage crew I'd been coming to rehearsals for weeks. Mr. Howitch had me sweeping the stage and standing in for cast members who were absent. He always said, "Laura, I want you in my theater as much as you can be here." So far, with my jaw wired shut for six weeks and then the recovery time after that, I hadn't been much use to him as a singer or an actor. But for some reason he still believed in me.

I wonder if HE knows what's going on with Mrs. I., I thought. *They're, like, best friends.*

"Hey you—Duffy."

Benjamin was looking from me to his clipboard and back again. His upper lip was dotted with perspiration.

"Sorry." I was still talking like I had sandpaper in my throat.

"You're going to have to be sharp back here, people," he said like a drill sergeant.

I heard a little gasp beside me and looked down to see one of the freshman girls who always sat at the table next to ours during lunch. I noticed she was already wearing the black pants and long-sleeved T-shirt we didn't have to wear until we started using lights and stuff. She even had a black scarf tied around her very-blond bob. She looked like she was more neurotic about the rules than I was. Her eyes had now grown to the size of soupspoons.

"Don't let him scare you," I whispered to her.

"I just know I'm gon' totally mess up," she whispered back.

She had one of those native-to-the-Panhandle accents that added several syllables to every word. Bless her heart, she sounded absolutely tragic over the whole thing.

"All right, I need two of you to carry out this flat at the end of act one," Benjamin was saying.

"She and I will do it," I said, pointing to Little Freshman.

"Okay, Duffy and Partlowe."

Benjamin made a note with a flourish of his gel pen, and she looked up at me as if I'd just rescued her from the bottom of the Gulf.

"Thank you," she breathed.

"What's your first name, Partlowe?" I said.

"Eve," she said.

"I'm—"

"Laura. I already know."

She scrunched up her shoulders and gave me a smile. She had those rich lips like you see on models in *Seventeen*, and she probably didn't even know it.

After that I got absorbed in the run-through and put Mrs. Isaacsen into the back of my mind. I had enough to do just trying to keep Eve from knocking over the entire set with her elbows and taking out several items every time she passed the prop table. When we left for the night she told me I'd saved her life.

Rehearsal didn't run that late; when I got home, Mom, Dad, and Bonnie were piling into the van in the driveway.

"We're going for ice cream!" Bonnie said, hair chattering.

"Come with, huh?" Mom said. "Some sherbet would feel good on your throat."

I knew it was the last step before she said, *I'm taking you to the doctor.* She still wasn't convinced that it didn't hurt, even though I'd told her so at least five thousand times.

"Sure," I said. "I could use a hot fudge sundae. Maybe two."

"If Laurie gets two sundaes, then I get two," Bonnie said. She was buckled in, but she still managed to bounce several inches off the seat.

"You'll vurp," I said.

"What's vurp?" Her brows knotted suspiciously.

"It's when you burp, only you almost vomit."

"Laura!" Mom said.

"It's a Celeste-ism," I said.

"That explains it," Dad said.

I only ordered one hot fudge sundae and was about to dig into it when Bonnie said, "Aren't we going to pray?"

"We prayed at supper," Dad said. He winked at me over Bonnie's head.

"We're gonna eat—we gotta pray." She stuck out two chubby hands. We latched on, and she launched into "God is great" at about half the normal speed but twice the necessary volume.

Are you getting this, God? I thought. *She's slowed it way down for you in case you have trouble keeping up.*

When Bonnie finished with a resounding "Amen!" that was louder than the milk shake machine, I raised my head to make sure my entire sundae hadn't melted into a puddle.

My eyes landed on a guy standing not three feet away.

It was Duck.

chapterfive

For some reason seeing Duck staring back at me with a giant frozen coffee drink in his hand was like watching a train wreck. I didn't want to see him, but I couldn't look away. And I also couldn't stop my already rosy cheeks from burning into the next shade on the embarrassment scale. The only thing that kept me from diving under the table was the fact that he looked pretty embarrassed himself. He gave me a quick wave and sprinted for the door.

I turned to my sundae and started shoveling it in.

Okay, so what was THAT about? I asked myself through the ensuing brain freeze. *Why was HE embarrassed?*

I knew immediately, of course. Seeing us pray, right there in front of God and everybody, obviously made him feel weird.

So much for him, then. A guy that's turned off by prayer—I don't think so.

Not that I really give a flip anyway. I am SO not interested in boys right now.

Those were all the "right" thoughts, but they didn't give me that reassuring you-are-so-GOOD feeling. As a matter of fact, I actually felt a little twist. Where did I get off judging him because he was weirded out by our bowed heads? I'd been the same way myself not six months before.

Hello! Maybe I still am? Whose cheeks turned redder just now?

One thing was for sure: Duck didn't think I was hot anymore.

But what I couldn't figure out was why I was disappointed. I'd said *NO GUYS* to myself and everybody else who would listen—and I meant it. So what was the deal?

✳   ✳   ✳

It took me until the next morning when I met the BFFs before school to get it.

I was running late because I'd had a—discussion—with my mother about her wanting me to see a doctor. I'd backed out the kitchen door, pulling a thermometer out of my mouth, and croaking at her, "It's always worse when I first get up, Mom—and it doesn't hurt!" It really didn't, not even when I tried to sing with the radio on my drive to school.

When I arrived, there was a table set up in front of the main office where people could sign up to run for student government offices. It was only 7:15 in the morning, but kids who normally didn't drag themselves in until halfway through first period, coffee in hand, were there vying for places in line like it was the place to buy tickets for an Avril Lavigne concert. To say student government was the socially "in" thing to do at 'Nama High was an understatement.

"Dude, Duffy," Celeste said to me when I'd swum through the crowd to get to their waiting hugs. "I was about to call you. I thought you forgot."

"No way," I said. I threaded my arms past Joy Beth and Trent and hugged Stevie's neck. "This is huge for you."

"It's just the sign-ups," Stevie said. "I don't know why I'm so nervous."

She did look strangely rattled. Her eyes were restless, darting all around like they were looking for a getaway car.

"Next in line, please."

That came from Mrs. Underwood, the large vice principal in charge of student activities, who was sitting behind the table. I'd never actually been this close to the woman before, but from afar I'd noticed that she had the biggest feet I'd ever seen on a female. Now that I was only a yard away from her, the rest of her seemed larger than life, too, including the 'do, which was cemented into place with hairspray. She even dwarfed Joy Beth.

But when she saw Stevie standing before her, her square face softened into a smile.

"Stephanie!" she said. "I am so glad to see you here. I was afraid you weren't going to run."

Joy Beth gave Stevie a small shove toward the table.

"I just decided to do it a couple days ago," Stevie said. All traces of freaking out had melted into the sheer authentic poise that made every adult want to trust Stevie with their car keys, their test answers, their innermost secrets.

"Good decision," Mrs. Underwood said. "Here's your packet. You'll need to give a copy of the teacher recommendation form to every one of your teachers and your counselor, fill out the application, and get 50 signatures from students who trust you to run a clean race."

"Piece of cake," Celeste said. "She'll have it all done by the end of the day."

Mrs. Underwood let her glance slide over Celeste and rest on Stevie again. "I don't doubt it, but you do have until a week from Friday."

"Yes, ma'am," Stevie said. "Thank you."

She turned from the table with us, her campaign team, loyally tagging along behind her.

"Stephanie," Mrs. Underwood said.

Stevie did an about-face with a swirl of her hair.

"I'm so glad you're doing this. I think you can turn student government around."

By the time we rounded the corner and headed for the locker hall, Celeste looked like she was about to do a triple lutz with a double toe jump. But we'd only gone about three steps when another group seemed to materialize right out of the trophy cases and stand in front of us. I almost walked up Stevie's calves when she stopped a few inches short of Gigi's nose.

I could hear Joy Beth groaning under her breath behind me.

"Steves!" Gigi said. "You're running for president, too?"

The synthetic honey was so thick, I wanted to vurp.

"How cool is that?" said the massively curled girl beside her. What had Stevie said her name was? Wuthering? Keating? Something pretentious.

"Do you know Fielding?" Gigi said, putting her arm around the much-shorter chick.

"We've met," Stevie said.

Her voice was pulled-back, cool. Gigi, on the other hand, was oozing like a tube of coconut oil.

"She's my campaign manager. This is going to be such a blast!"

"Uh-huh," Stevie said. "I plan to have a good time with it."

Gigi pushed her expression into something resembling acid indigestion. "You don't mind that I'm running, do you?"

"Stevie might not mind," Celeste muttered to me. "But I do."

"It's fine with me," Stevie said. "I just didn't know you were allowed to be involved in activities already."

If that was meant to pry out the real Gigi, it worked. Her eyes glittered with unmistakable hatred. But only for a second or two. She recovered like a seasoned actress.

"I've completed all my punishments," she said. "And even though they were totally unfair, I sucked it up. Mrs. Underwood and Mr. Wylie and Mrs. Vaughn all said I can participate in anything I want to now."

"Isn't that special?" Celeste said between her teeth.

Gigi's eyes hit Celeste and me, drilling right into our foreheads. I didn't waver—I didn't even feel like hiding behind Joy Beth. Gigi had brought everything on herself, and we would see the last of her if she tried to mess up the election. I just looked right back at her until she found her fake smile again and turned back to Stevie.

"Did you know there's nobody else running for president but the two of us?"

"That pretty much narrows it down," Stevie said.

"Well, good luck," Gigi said. "May the best girl win."

And then she deposited a look on Stevie that clearly said there was only one reason she was running at all: She wanted to take her down.

Gigi and Fielding swept away, greeting every person they saw between us and the sign-up table as if they'd been her kindred spirits since kindergarten. Joy Beth watched them go, her fists opening and closing at her sides.

"You okay?" I said to Stevie.

She nodded, but there was something painful stirring in her eyes.

"You are SO not going to let her get to you, are you?" Celeste said. "I swear, if she tries anything, I am gonna be all over her—"

"No!" Stevie said. "I'm going to run a clean race, and there's nothing she can do to me."

"Exactly," I said. "Who's even going to vote for her anyway? Everybody knows what she's done to us. She's not the queen bee anymore."

"Oh, yeah?" Joy Beth jerked her head toward the sign-up table. "You coulda fooled me."

Gigi was currently surrounded by the same group of kids she'd hung out with before she had, as Mrs. I. once put it, "become despised and rejected by the administration." Any minute now I expected her to start signing autographs. I really did want to vurp.

"They're such fakes, Stevie," Celeste said. "Everybody knows that. Just chill. You're SO gonna win."

Stevie nodded, but her eyes tilted down at the corners, the tiny places on her face where she couldn't hide a certain sadness.

"They all used to be YOUR friends, huh?" I said.

"Who needs them?" Celeste said. "You've got us now."

Stevie tilted her chiseled chin up. "I'm right where I want to be. I just hate it that they turned out to be such—posers. I used to spend all my time with them—I shared all my stuff."

"I hate it FOR you," I said. "You don't deserve that kind of treatment from people. You're too good."

"I'm not that good. I just care too much."

We stood there for a long, quiet moment, even while the racket of the bell and the sway of pushing and shoving students went on chaotically around us. Our strong, confident Stevie looked so vulnerable. She actually still cared about those people, and it was wasted on them.

I breathed in a little God. *It's not wasted on us,* I suddenly wanted to say to her. *You can never love us too much.*

And then it struck me. She DID care about me, enough to give up the whole prom dream if I didn't get a date.

THAT, I knew, was what that whole thing with Duck was about—why I was disappointed that I was an embarrassment to him. Stevie and Celeste wanted him for a prom date for me, and if I went with him, they could both do the thing with the dresses and the limos and the French manicures.

But Duck wasn't the answer. I didn't want to be somebody's worst nightmare because I prayed.

✳ ✳ ✳

Stevie was still bummed at lunchtime. She pushed her Caesar salad around with her fork and never actually took a bite.

"You're letting that Gigi chick get to you, aren't you?" Celeste said. "Man, Stevie, you're giving her what she wants!"

"You can take her," Joy Beth said.

I wasn't sure whether she meant in the election or in hand-to-hand combat.

"I just wanted to run for president because it's the right thing to do," Stevie said. "I have all these great ideas—I really can turn student government around."

"And you will," Celeste said. "Because you're gonna win."

"But that's just it. Now it isn't going to be about my ideas or about me being the right person for the job." Stevie planted her chin on her folded hands. Even her hair was drooping. "Now there's going to be all this mudslinging, and I'm going to have to watch my back every second. You know this is going to get ugly."

"With that chick involved, yeah," Trent said.

"Maybe I should just stick with defending people with the pledge," Stevie said, "instead of trying to get elected president. If Gigi's going to turn this into a—"

"Wait!" I said.

"Okay, stand by," Celeste said. "Duffy's got that look."

"Uh-oh," Trent said.

I swiveled around so I could get right into Stevie's face.

"This IS about the pledge," I said. "You're part of the solution to end the hate in this school. You'll speak up when other people are showing their ignorance. You'll do it like a caring person—all the things that are in the pledge." I waved a hand over the table. "And we're all in it with you."

"So it's like the pledge is for Stevie," Joy Beth said.

"That's totally it," I said.

Celeste grinned as she readjusted the red-white-and-blue scarf she had tied around her ponytail. It was the first time I'd noticed she was wearing a patriotic ensemble. Of course.

"Who knew?" she said. "It's like we took the pledge just for this. How cool is that?"

"Do you really think so?" Stevie said.

"I absolutely do," I said. "We won't tear anybody down. We'll just pray for Gigi and them when they're being stupid, and we'll go on with our mission, which is getting you elected so you can make a difference."

"You're gonna cry, aren't you?" Celeste said to Stevie.

"Aw, man, don't cry," Trent said. "I can't handle crying."

Stevie laughed at him, tears streaming down her face. I looked over to see Eve and her little friend openly watching us from the next table, mouths agape.

"Hey," I said to them. "Stevie's running for president of student government. You want to sign her signature sheet?"

Eve immediately pawed through her backpack for a pen.

"Dude," Celeste murmured to me. "What kind of threat have you got over that child?"

While Eve and her dutiful friend scribbled their names on Stevie's sheet, I sat there feeling pretty good about my sweet self once more.

We did it, God, I thought. *We've found our mission.*

Huh. Little did I know.

✳   ✳   ✳

I was still on a high about it the next day. We had Stevie all pumped up, and she was out there coaxing signatures out of people with little more than a smile. It seemed to me she was made for the job, and we were made to get her there.

I guess I was feeling my Cheerios, as my dad always said, when the discussion started in history second period. Once a week Mr. Beecher brought up a topic that he wanted us to debate, and that day it was the rise in violence in American society.

As usual I was mostly listening, since in an honors class there are always plenty of people vying for extra credit points. But I found myself pulling up from the doodling I was doing on my binder when I realized that something different was shooting everybody's hands up in the air today. And it had nothing to do with their GPAs.

"I don't think there's any more violence than there ever was," this one kid named Jeremy said. "We just hear about it more because we're more technologically advanced."

"You mean the media," Mr. Beecher said.

"Sure—and the Internet. Now it's just out in the open that when you get right down to it, we're all basically animals."

"Real nice, Jeremy," Allison Mack said. "Now I'm a gorilla or something."

"No, Jeremy's the gorilla," another girl put in. The way she giggled, I was sure she had received that information firsthand.

"We ARE animals," Jeremy said. "The civilized behaviors we have are learned, but basically we're just as base as your average baboon."

I looked at Stevie. She was biting her lower lip.

"I gotta agree with that," said Jeremy's echo, Mike. He was long on going whichever way the smart kids were headed and short on original thought. "You get two girls havin' a turf war over some guy, and they might as well be a coupla alley cats."

There was a unanimous chorus from the males in the class. Stevie and I rolled our eyes at each other.

"So what's our point here?" Mr. Beecher said. He was all but licking his chops.

"People are violent," Jeremy said, his voice sounding like a dial tone. "Always have been. Always will be. There's nothing you can do about it."

"I'm not violent!" Allison said.

"You haven't started dating yet, have you?" Giggle Girl said to her.

It was the girls' turn for a round of knowing laughter. Even I had to admit there was something to that. At that point I was ready to strangle Jeremy.

"I'm serious!" Allison said. "Things tick me off, but I don't go around taking people out with an AK-47."

"Like I said, self-control is learned behavior." Jeremy shrugged off her ignorance. "But if you really got pushed hard enough, you'd snap. It's human nature."

Mr. Beecher was playing with his moustache. "So you're saying we shouldn't be concerned about kids shooting up a high school?"

By now I was leaning so far out of the desk to see Jeremy, I was in danger of falling out.

"It's just part of life," Jeremy said. "We can try to control it, but we can't get all wigged out when it happens. We either accept it or put tranquilizers in the drinking water."

"Sounds good to me!" said somebody on the other side of the room.

Amid the follow-up laughter my hand found its way into the air. Mr. Beecher nodded at me.

"We're not animals," I said. "We were put here to take CARE of the animals, well, the whole earth really. We might have the urge to be violent, but that's only when we refuse to take the responsibility we've been given as human beings."

"By who?" Jeremy said.

His eyes had grown skinny on either side of his nose. I felt like I was looking at a hatchet.

"By God," I said. "We're made in his image. And I think when we live up to that, we don't have the urge to blow somebody away."

"Or if we have it," Stevie said, "we have somebody to answer to who's bigger than we are."

Jeremy's mouth jerked into a crooked line. "Oh, so you're saying we should all join hands and sing 'Kum-Ba-Yah' so all wars will cease—"

"Oh, don't be a moron," Stevie said. "You know that's not what we're saying."

"Let's do this without the name-calling, Stephanie," Mr. Beecher said.

"Let me get this straight," Allison said. "Jeremy can call us monkeys, which we're not, but we can't call him a moron, which he is?"

While Mr. Beecher was sorting that out, I looked at Stevie. She was blowing out air with her bottom lip, sending her bangs up like floating feathers.

"They don't get it," I said.

"And they never will," Stevie said. "There's no point in arguing with them."

"I got something to say," Jeremy called above the din.

"Go for it, Jeremy," Mr. Beecher said.

Jeremy had me in his sights.

"You have a right to your opinion," he said, "but if we're going to have an intelligent discussion, anything you put out there should be based on fact."

"Fact?" I said. "Or truth?"

"Same thing."

"Okay, then—my beliefs are based on truths, which you say are also considered facts, so what's your point?"

The room thickened with silence.

"You're talking about the Bible," Jeremy said.

"The Bible. Christian tradition. My own relationship with God."

"Do you believe in evolution?" he said.

"We're not talking about evolution." I leaned further out. "We're talking about the nature of human beings and how we can overcome sin."

Jeremy practically climbed up onto his desktop. "See, there's where you're wrong," he said. "There's no such thing as something being a sin in and of itself. It all depends on the situation." He all but added *little girl* on the end of the sentence.

You are SO wrong, I wanted to say to him, *because I'm about to sin right now when I tell you you're an absurd, small-minded, little creep—*

The bell rang, and the class blew out of there like a volcanic eruption. Jeremy collected his books, walked past me, and—I am so serious—patted the top of my head. ONLY because there's a God did I NOT reach up and snatch every hair out of his condescending scalp.

"Bless his heart, he's such a jerk," Stevie said to me.

"Tell me about it," I said.

"Ladies, a word."

We both looked up at Mr. Beecher, who was standing over us with his arms folded across his chest. There were two distinct rings of perspiration seeping from the underarms of his shirt.

"It's okay, Mr. B.," Stevie said. "We've been through this before. We can handle it."

"I'm not worried about you two," he said. "I just don't want a repeat of the discussion we just had."

Something uneasy began to creep up my spinal column.

"I certainly respect your Christian beliefs," he said. "I'm a Christian myself. But I want you to be very careful about expressing them in the classroom. It isn't always appropriate."

"Why?" I said.

He sighed. "Because this is a captive audience. Anyone who is offended can't just walk out of the room."

"But what Jeremy said offended ME," I said. "And I can't walk out of the room either."

Irritation etched Mr. Beecher's face. "He was stating an opinion. You have to learn to live with the differences people express."

"But I was—"

"You were preaching. There's a difference."

Then he turned away, signaling the end of the conversation. I left the room feeling like his thumbprint was carved into my head.

"We're going to Mrs. I.," Stevie said. "And we're going now."

chaptersix

M rs. I.'s door was closed when we got there. I started to knock, but Stevie curled her fingers around my wrist just as I heard raised voices behind the door.

At first I couldn't make out the exact words. But I could tell that the owner of the male voice was NOT in a good mood. And judging by her muffled syllables, neither was Mrs. Isaacsen.

As Stevie and I stood there, our ears practically pressed to the door, droplets of sentences bled through.

"It is NOT a prayer meeting—"

"—airing your religious convictions—"

"I meet them where they are!"

"Then meet them in church—"

Stevie and I would have stood there until somebody threw a punch if Michelle hadn't come up behind us and said, "They told me to tell you to move on."

I knew I had questions plastered all over my face, but Michelle said, "I don't know anything."

It was hard to tell whether she did or not, but I knew we wouldn't be getting anything out of her.

The things I'd overheard nagged at me all day like a low-grade fever that refused to break. Even processing it with Stevie until we both ran out of things to say—which was a LOT of processing—and running it by the

BFFs during lunch didn't ease my mind. We had an extra scene-changing rehearsal that day after school; and by the time I got there, my thoughts were so tangled up I could barely remember what play we were doing.

Who had been in there with Mrs. Isaacsen, chewing her out?

The discussion was obviously about something Christian she was doing. Was there suddenly some kind of vendetta against churchgoers?

It had to be somebody with power over her, or she would have told whoever it was to get over himself. Mrs. I. didn't put up with people throwing themselves around that way.

But what if it WAS someone powerful? What if she was actually in some kind of trouble? What if—?

That line of thinking put my whole brain in a square knot. And that's the state I was in when Eve and I practiced a scene change at the end of act one. As we carried a flat onto the stage, she dropped her end. On my foot.

"Dang!" I hissed at her hoarsely. "Could you pay attention?"

"I'm sorry—"

"Just pick it up—pick it up—PICK IT UP!"

Although my voice was all but disappearing, Benjamin barked at us to chill out and get the scene changed. I sighed in Eve's face and dragged the flat into place by myself.

"I'm sorry I yelled at you," I whispered to her later when I found her cowering near the prop table.

"Oh, it's okay—"

"No it's not. I was upset about something else, and I took it out on you. I shouldn't have done that."

"It didn't bother me," she said.

"SHHHHHHH!"

I wasn't sure whether Benjamin was spewing sweat or saliva at us. I pulled Eve through the door and out into the stairwell.

"It did bother you," I said. "Sometimes I just mess up—I'm sorry."

"Oh." The little freshman face broke into a rosy smile. "I think you're cool anyway."

What that kid saw in me I had no idea. I talked to Stevie about it as we walked to her car after rehearsal ended, our beach bags in hand.

The night before, Stevie, Celeste, and I had decided we should go to the beach after my play rehearsal ended and catch some sun while we did our homework. It had been Stevie's idea, naturally. She said it might be healing for my throat. Besides, she could never get tan enough, even when Celeste told her she was going to look like a leather briefcase before she was 30.

"It's like Eve thinks I'm the Virgin Mary or something," I said. "Then when I yelled at her, she just, like, crumbled."

"Well, you are the Virgin Laura." Stevie's grin was sly.

"You know what I mean! And after that thing in history—and whatever's going on with Mrs. I.—I just feel like I'm not handling any of it right. I feel—stupid!"

Stevie slung her bag onto her other shoulder and put her arm around mine. "Bless your heart," she said. "I don't think you're stupid— and neither does God."

"Can you people never give it a rest?"

We both turned to see Gigi and Fielding leaning against a white Mustang convertible, top down.

There wasn't a sign of that "may the best girl win" attitude in Gigi's eyes today. Evidently she saved that for times when her potential voters were present to witness it.

"What needs a rest?" Stevie said.

"The whole God thing," Gigi said.

I thought I saw her give Fielding a minute nudge.

"I hardly know you," Fielding said. "But I can already see how holier-than-thou y'all are."

Her *y'all* sounded unnatural. *It's probably part of the Gigi clone program*, I thought.

Stevie cocked her head at Fielding, matching her tress for tress. "We don't try to be holier than anybody," she said. "If that's the way you see it, maybe you've been spending too much time with someone who ISN'T trying to be holy." She turned to me. "You ready, Duffy?"

After that I couldn't get myself cheered up, not even sitting on the cotton-white sand at St. Andrew's Bay, one of my favorite spots on the planet. Not even with the sun soaking through my SPF 40 like a soothing hand or with the water lapping up against the jetties and the dunes with their heads of pampas grass hair that waved hypnotically in the breeze. Not even with Celeste handing out sandwiches that I knew would be to-die-for delicious—if I had any appetite.

"I'm serious now," I said. "What do you guys think is going on with Mrs. I.? She had her office door closed all day."

"We really need to talk to her," Stevie said. "I want to know what my rights are—you know, whether I can even mention God in the classroom."

"You gonna talk about God in your campaign?" Celeste said. She leaned back and licked some mustard off her forearm.

"Well—I mean, God is what I'm all about."

"Then we definitely need to find out what the rules are," I said. "I don't want somebody like Mr. Beecher getting in your face again."

"I'll call Trent tonight," she said. "He'll get on the Internet."

Celeste snickered. "And he'll tell us more than we really want to know."

I felt a little better, but there was something nagging at me, and I couldn't quite hear what it was.

✳   ✳   ✳

My eyes were definitely opened the next morning, though. When I got out of my car, I saw about 20 people marching around on the school lawn where everybody gathered on warm mornings before the bell rang. More people than usual were out there, and I could feel that something's-gonna-happen energy before I even got close enough to read the protest signs they were flashing around.

I spotted Trent and Joy Beth at the edge of the crowd and hurried toward them. Whatever was happening, it looked pretty organized. The picketers were walking slowly, unemotionally, and somebody else was calmly passing out sheets of paper to the students who showed up to gape.

One of the sign-carrying kids was Duck. His face was a bilious red, and his head was lowered, as if he were afraid someone might recognize him. I almost hadn't.

He looks embarrassed, I thought. *Maybe he just always looks embarrassed.*

"Hey," I croaked when I got to Trent and Joy Beth. "What's this about?"

Trent pointed to the sign Duck was holding.

PROTECT SEPARATION OF CHURCH AND STATE

"What?" I whispered to Joy Beth.
She just grunted and nodded to another sign.

PROTECT YOUR FIRST AMENDMENT RIGHTS! PROTEST PREACHING IN PUBLIC SCHOOLS!

Gigi Palmer turned her head and smiled that plastic smile at me as she carried it past me.

chapterseven

By the time Celeste and Stevie joined us, I'd picked up one of the fliers somebody had already dropped on the ground.

ACCORDING TO THE FIRST AMENDMENT OF THE CONSTITUTION, IT'S AGAINST THE LAW TO FORCE RELIGION ON ANYONE. STAND UP FOR YOUR RIGHTS!

"They are NOT serious," Celeste said, reading the flier over my shoulder.

"They look pretty serious to me," Trent said. He pointed to a trio of boys—all of them jocks—who were hooking up a portable loudspeaker to a microphone.

"This is unreal," Stevie said.

I looked at the crowd of kids that was swelling by the second. Several of them were calling out, "Sweet!" and, "That's what I'm talkin' about!" When I peered more closely, I caught a glimpse of someone standing behind them. A guy with a saddened expression—and a ponytail.

A gasp slipped from me.

"Yeah—exactly," Stevie said.

But she was nodding toward the microphone where Gigi was climbing up onto a box amid catcalls, which she was apparently enjoying.

"Somebody please tell me she isn't going to make a speech," Celeste said.

I jerked back to the crowd and tried to find Ponytail Boy again, but he was gone—if he had ever really been there at all.

"Just so you know," Gigi was saying—too loudly—into the microphone. There was a feedback screech, and about six guys leaped to correct the problem.

"Get over it," Joy Beth muttered.

"We want this to be a peaceful demonstration," Gigi went on. "We simply wish to be heard above the preaching that's been going on at 'Nama Beach High, which is absolutely unconstitutional."

"What?" Celeste said. Her voice outdid the PA system by several decibels.

"Shut UP, Celeste," Trent said through his teeth.

"When SHE does," Celeste hissed through hers.

"My biggest concern—" Gigi was saying.

"Is that you might break a nail," Stevie said close to my ear.

"—is that there are teachers involved in undermining the constitution."

"Teachers?" I whispered.

Joy Beth jerked her chin toward a sign carried by that Jeremy kid from history class:

MRS. ISAACSEN SHOULD READ HER CONSTITUTION!

He was holding it up like it was suddenly his mission in life. But from the way he was leering at Allison as she walked beside him with her hand in his back pocket, it was obvious that his true mission had nothing to do with the First Amendment.

"Now that is just WRONG!"

A ripple went through the crowd, and everybody's neck craned to see who was about to make this little demonstration more interesting. I'd croaked it—out loud—almost before I thought it. And that wasn't all of it.

"Mrs. Isaacsen never tried to push anything down our throats!" I said. "She's a great Christian, but she's not going around selling it!"

"I said I wanted this to be a peaceful demonstration," Gigi said. Her voice was a study in righteous disappointment.

"So we're supposed to stand here and swallow a bunch of bunk?" Celeste shouted at her.

"NO!" Joy Beth hollered. She raised a fist in the air. Then she grabbed poor Trent's hand and held it up with hers.

What went down after that resembled a practiced drill, as though the administrators had been preparing for just such an occasion. Mr. Stennis, the vice principal for discipline, took the microphone from Gigi—with an apology—and told the crowd to go on to class.

Mrs. Vaughn, the academic vice principal, put her arm around Gigi—as though this incident would surely cause an emotional breakdown—and helped her down from the box as about 13 boys crowded around to offer their support as well.

Then suddenly Mrs. Underwood towered behind us. She put one man-sized hand on my back, the other on Celeste's, and said, "Let's go, ladies." The jerk of the cement hairdo included Joy Beth and Trent.

She pushed us through the crowd—who were all either staring as if we were naked or taking shots like, "Busted!" and, "Hey, thanks a lot." Even when Jeremy said, "Jesus freaks," Mrs. Underwood acted like she didn't hear him.

When we got inside the building, she steered us toward the main office. Stevie was on our heels.

"Wait out here," Mrs. Underwood said to us. "Stephanie, go on to class. You do NOT need to be involved in this."

But Stevie shook her head.

"We're all in it together," she said. "I want to go in."

"In," it was apparent by now, was going to be the office of Mr. Wylie, the principal. With so many vice principals on staff nobody went to HIS office unless they were about to be made a Rhodes Scholar or expelled from school. I was pretty sure this wasn't about a scholarship, and my mouth turned to fiberglass.

The only other BFF who even looked concerned was Trent. His little mouth was pulled in so far, I was afraid he was going to swallow his lips. Celeste, on the other hand, looked like she was ready to take out the next person who crossed her, although she would have to stand in line behind Joy Beth. Even Stevie had her shoulders squared and was the picture of courage. But they were all looking to me. I took in a big ol' gulp of air and hoped God came with it.

"They can't suspend us just for expressing our opinions," I said. My voice had gone back into its frog-like mode. I had no idea how I'd been able to speak so clearly across the schoolyard.

"Did you have to EXPRESS yours like you were trying to incite a riot?" Trent said to Celeste.

"Did you find anything on the Internet, Trent?" I said quickly.

"Now would be a good time for you to start spittin' out some facts," Celeste said.

Mr. Wylie appeared just then and nodded at Mrs. Underwood to usher us all into his office. When he followed us in and shut the door behind him, I was grateful Mrs. Underwood didn't join us.

Our principal was a short man with a slight build, but he was solid. His white dress shirt fit him well enough to reveal that he obviously worked out on a regular basis. He wore his silver-tipped dark hair in a severe buzz-cut style and had the military posture to match.

He jabbed a finger toward three faux leather loveseats arranged in a U at one end of his office and said, "Have a seat."

We sank down in unison—all but Celeste, who had to be told twice. Stevie kept a hand on Celeste's arm after that, which I appreciated. This was SO not the time for Celeste to go ballistic.

God, I prayed—with my eyes open and glued to Mr. Wylie's grim face—*something is so messed up here. Please—give me a word—just a word.*

I felt a narrow ribbon of peace slide through me. This was, after all, a chance for us to put the pledge into action. We could handle this like Christians.

"Is there a problem, Mr. Wylie?" I said.

"Ya think?" Celeste said. "They don't drag you in here to ask how your day's going."

I put a hand on Celeste's other arm. "We're not going to do that, " I said to her.

Celeste held a debate with her face for a couple of seconds before she sat back on the couch. "Then you'd better do the talking, Duffy," she said.

"How about if I do the talking?" Mr. Wylie said. His gaze bore down on me. "I don't like what happened out there, and I hope you don't either."

He didn't give us a chance to answer.

"Gigi Palmer came to me late yesterday afternoon," he said, "asking for permission to have a peaceful demonstration regarding some concerns she has about the school. I told her it was fine as long as no one stirred up any trouble." The gaze drilled deeper into me. He didn't have to say he thought I'd been out there with a giant wooden spoon. "I also told her that the minute there was any resistance, it would be over."

He was starting to remind me of a miniature Doberman.

"I wasn't trying to stir anything up," I said. "I was just standing up for Mrs. Isaacsen. She's the best person on the entire staff, and she doesn't deserve—"

"Mrs. Isaacsen?" he said.

"Kids were carrying signs about her not upholding the constitution," Stevie said.

"Let's keep the focus on you people, shall we?" Mr. Wylie folded his arms across his chest like he was Arnold Schwarzenegger. "You certainly have a right to your own beliefs and opinions, but you may not proselytize on this campus."

"I don't know what that is," Celeste said. "But I know I don't do it."

"It means trying to make converts," Trent said. His voice was so faint it was quieter than mine.

"Were we breaking a law out there?" Stevie said.

Joy Beth gave Trent a major jab in the side with her elbow. He slid down, squeaking against the faux leather, but he couldn't escape Joy Beth's killer gaze.

"Did you find out some stuff?" Celeste said to him.

Trent nodded miserably.

"Were we breaking the law?" Stevie said again.

"We aren't in violation of the Federal Equal Access Act," Trent said through a small hole.

"What's that?" Stevie was using her softest voice—the one most guys would go into battle for. Too bad Trent wasn't most guys.

"It means most student-led, noncurriculum-related clubs have to be allowed to organize in public high schools," he said. "Even religious ones."

Mr. Wylie recrossed his arms impatiently. "First of all, you weren't AT a private club meeting—it was a public demonstration. Second of all, I was never informed that there was such a club here at Panama Beach High. And you mentioned Mrs. Isaacsen. A noncurricular club like this can't be sponsored by a teacher."

The BFFs all looked at me as if they'd been shot.

"She doesn't sponsor us!" I said. "And it isn't really a club. Aren't we allowed to—"

"Look, people," he said. "I don't want any trouble in my school." He focused his eyes directly on me. "And you, Miss Duffy, have a reputation for finding it."

"I was the one who got everybody going out there just now," Celeste said. She flashed a white-toothed smile at Mr. Wylie. "I got a big mouth sometimes."

"All you need is a little provocation—isn't that right?" he said. His eyes were still on me. "I don't want a repeat of this. That's all. My secretary will give you passes to class."

Somehow we were shown out of the office and handed yellow admit slips. I was so confused I couldn't even decide what books to get out of my locker.

"What just happened in there, Duffy?" Stevie said to me.

"I have no idea. We HAVE to talk to Mrs. I."

I had never needed her more. But when we all showed up at her office for activity period, there was a sign on the door:

NO COUNSELING GROUP TODAY.
MRS. ISAACSEN HAS BEEN CALLED AWAY.

I turned around to locate Michelle, who was filing papers at a nearby cabinet.

"Don't ask me," she said. The pitch of her voice was raised several octaves, which meant that was all she was going to say about it.

K.J. flung her bag over her shoulder. It hit her in the back, right where her bandana-print halter top stopped. Mrs. Isaacsen's "call" must have happened before K.J. got dressed that morning.

"All right, give it up, K.J.," Celeste said. "What's this about?"

K.J.'s eyes narrowed to points. "Like I know. But I bet it's about that demonstration. Her name was all over those signs."

"I hate this," Stevie said. She raked a hand through her hair.

"I just hope she doesn't get fired over it," K.J. said. "Now THAT would be something worth protesting."

"We weren't the ones who started that whole mess," Celeste said. "That was Gigi's gig—and it wasn't about religion. It was about putting Stevie down."

"Whatever," K.J. said, and she turned on an almost-stiletto heel and strutted off, thighs exposed.

"Okay, that skirt is out of control," Stevie said.

But my mind was far from K.J.'s wardrobe. I had a knot in my stomach to match the tangle in my brain. I didn't even know what to pray for, so for the rest of the day I tried to just let God breathe into me. It was amazing that I didn't get run over when I was walking to my car in the parking lot after school. As it was I didn't see Joy Beth until she was beside me, her face set like concrete.

"You okay?" I said. "You aren't having an insulin reaction, are you?"

She shook her head. Her hair was tucked firmly behind her ears, as if she'd been preparing to lay something on me and she didn't want anything to get in the way.

"I can't get in trouble like that again, or Coach Powell said I'd be off the swim team," she said. She looked at the toe of her Nike as she dragged it back and forth across the asphalt. "I can't do anything religious on campus."

"So—I guess baptizing people in the pool is out of the question," I said.

She didn't laugh.

"Joy Beth, what's this about?"

She swung her head in rhythm with her foot. "Coach just says I can't do anything that's gonna give the swim team a bad name. Not that we would—but HE thinks so." For the first time she looked at me, and her eyes were wet. "I have to swim, Duffy. I've wanted this all my life, and now I have a chance. I can't—"

"Of course you can't," I said. "I promise I won't ask you to walk on water or feed the five thousand with your bologna sandwich until AFTER the Olympics."

She still didn't laugh. Neither did I.

"You do what you have to do," I said.

"I think God wants me to swim."

"Then do it."

I patted her hefty arm, and she nodded before she walked away, her face aimed toward the pavement again.

What just happened, God? I prayed. *I am SO confused.*

Which was probably why I found a parchment envelope waiting for me when I went back to my locker before heading home. I didn't have to open it to know it was from my Secret Admirer. And I didn't even struggle over who he might be. I'd seen Ponytail Boy that morning at the demonstration. He was back, which meant I really must be in trouble.

What I pulled out of the envelope was not a note but a card—a wedding invitation.

Great, I thought, *he's marrying somebody else.*

Stuff from him always made me think weird things.

It was written in his usual perfect handwriting, and it said:

The honor of your presence, Laura Duffy,
is requested at your marriage.
Prepare to meet the bridegroom.
Oneness will be celebrated
with a banquet of praise.

Right about then I'd have taken him up on a marriage offer. Be swept away by a tall, slender man with an ethereal ponytail—or stay here and get clobbered from every side by people who didn't know prayer from a case of hyperventilation? Like that was a choice.

But he wasn't exactly proposing. I read the invitation three more times just to make sure, but there was no declaration of love. It kind of ticked me off.

I dug into my backpack, tore out a piece of paper, and grabbed a gel pen. I scrawled in less-than-perfect penmanship,

Dear Secret Admirer WITH the Ponytail,

First of all, don't think I don't know who you are. I saw you right here at school today. Secondly, I need your help—not these clue things. But since this is the way you work—please tell me where and when, and I'll be at the wedding. Just one thing— WHO am I marrying?!

Laura Duffy

I folded the paper again and again until it couldn't get any smaller. Then I stuffed it into my locker and slammed the door.

chaptereight

For the rest of the afternoon I thought I was going to crawl out of my skin. My tangle of thoughts had gotten too big for my brain, and they were now charging through my veins like liquid barbed wire.

I knew if I went to rehearsal in that condition, I would probably send poor little Eve into a mental hospital. So I drove downtown, parked the Mercedes, and walked down to the city pier.

It wasn't exactly your hip hangout, which was exactly why I liked to go there when I really wanted to meet God and do some serious talking. The pier was mostly filled with mothers with strollers and retired couples holding gnarled hands and talking about the weather in Celeste-like accents. I hurried past them into the Marina Store and out the back door to the padded chairs that nobody seemed to know about except a few gulls. I chose a blue-and-white striped one sitting right up against the deck railing and sank into it. I hoped that staring out at St. Andrew's Bay and letting the breeze untangle my mind would get me back to my peaceful place.

The bay was alive with Sunfish, tiny one-person sailboats with striped sails in primary colors, cutting through the water like cheerful little knives. The air pushed tiny ripples atop the water, in no hurry to get them to the Gulf. I closed my eyes and tried to be like them, moved only by the Spirit, in no hurry to get someplace until I knew where I was going.

I'm confused, God, I prayed. *I thought it would all be clear now that we've taken the pledge. Now that I'm so aware of your presence. Now that I have friends who know you and want you like I do. Now that I'm not alone.*

I breathed in—then out—over and over. My mind was still dark and knotty.

But there isn't a clear path for me to follow, God. It's like the sand's been kicked over it, and it's blowing in my face so I can't even see you in anything.

I can't talk about you in class.

I can't talk about you when other people are putting you down at school.

Joy Beth can't swim if she talks about you.

The holding back is making us all pointy and testy and obnoxious. Especially Celeste, as you know.

I sank further into the lounge chair. *Are you talking to ME, though? The Secret Admirer finally sent me a note—asking me to my own wedding. What is THAT about? And I can't even ask Mrs. I. about it because they have her tied and gagged, for all I know. She always came through with a piece of the sacred text that matched the clues my admirer teased me with. Now it just feels like there's no way to find out what you're saying to me.*

I opened my eyes and watched a gull catch a wind current and ride it like a wave, going with every capricious turn and curl.

Of course it whined, constantly. Bonnie had absolutely nothing on this bird. "Quit your cryin'," I whispered to it. "Most of us would kill to be able to fly, so I don't know what you're complaining about."

It landed on the top rung of the railing and cocked its head at me.

I got out of the chair and propped my elbows near it. "Y'all are the most neurotic of all animals," I told it.

It came two steps closer.

"Give it up. I don't have anything for you."

"Hey! Laura Duffy?"

I leaned out over the railing as a voice shouted up at me. There was a young man standing up to his ankles in white sand down on the beach, peering up at me from under the rim of a khaki ball cap. He had shoulders like a swimmer.

"It's Duck," he said. "Remember me?"

"Yeah," I said. I didn't add that I hadn't recognized him because it was the first time I'd seen him when he didn't look like he was about to die of humiliation.

In fact, the last time I'd seen him, he was carrying a sign for Gigi. I pulled back from the railing.

"Stay there." he said. "I'll buy you a Coke."

He didn't wait for an answer but disappeared into the building below. I could have made a hasty exit through the shop, but I didn't. I was suddenly sick of having to keep my mouth shut. Nobody could tell me I couldn't say anything I wanted out here on the bay.

So I waited, and Duck was there a few minutes later, handing me an icy-sweaty can of Coke and pulling a chair up next to mine. I tried not to look at him, but I couldn't help noticing that he was surprisingly tan for an almost redhead and that the T-shirt he'd pulled on still didn't hide the shoulders and the biceps and the pecs.

Stop, I told myself. *I am SO not going there.*

"Is Coke okay?" he said. "I didn't even ask you. I could get you a Sprite or something."

"Coke's fine," I said. I took a long drag out of the can so I didn't have to start the conversation. I knew if I opened my mouth right away, I'd blurt out something about the demonstration and his ignorance and my outrage. And then one of us would stomp away, and I'd be just as frustrated as ever.

He propped his long legs up on the railing. I couldn't help noticing that they were pretty muscular, too.

"Did y'all get in trouble over what happened this morning?" he said.

Soda fizz went straight up my nose.

"How ya doin'?" he said as I choked.

I nodded and waved him off.

"Should I take that as a yes?" he said.

"We just got a warning not to 'stir up any more trouble,'" I managed to get out. I gave him a pointed look. "Personally, I thought Gigi Palmer was the one stirring up trouble."

"She was."

"You were right in there with her!" I said.

"I don't even know her. Some chick just handed me a sign and told me to hold it."

"Didn't you read it?"

He ducked his head sheepishly. "Eventually. When I did, I put it down. I don't dig what she was doing out there."

"Which was?"

"Just trying to make a big scene so she'd get elected, I guess." He shrugged. "Like I said, I don't even know her. Do you?"

I studied the label on the can. "Too well. She made my life miserable for a while, me AND my friends. She can't be trusted."

"Ya think? I heard her gloating after Mrs. Underwood hauled y'all in. You'd think she already won the election."

"Not gonna happen," I said.

"Why? Does everybody know she's a witch?"

"No, unfortunately."

Duck turned his cap around backward and nodded. "I get it. Y'all are gonna make SURE they do."

"No—we're not." I swiveled sideways in the chair so I could look him full in the face. "Stevie's going to run a clean race—no mudslinging and no rumors. She's got great ideas, and she wants to be president so she can make them happen. You don't know Stevie—she's so incredible—"

I realized, as I chanced another drink out of the Coke can, that he was just sitting there, watching me out of eyes that were no longer at half-mast. They blinked large and blue, almost like a little boy staring at you in the grocery store.

Great, I thought. *I probably have a booger hanging out of my nose or something.*

I couldn't resist the urge to run a finger under my nostrils.

"So are you her campaign manager?" he said.

"Me? No. We're all working on it together."

"Who's we?"

"Me. Celeste Mancini. Joy Beth Barnes. Trent Newell. We're the main ones."

"The Jesus Freaks."

I slammed the can down on the arm of the chair.

"That's what they call you," Duck said. "Everybody who was standing there cheering that chick on. What was her name? Mimi?"

"Gigi," I said. I picked up the can and peered at him over the top of it. "What about you?"

"Y'mean do I think you're a Jesus Freak?"

I nodded.

"Yeah, probably. Who else would be, like, so unconcerned about what people thought that she'd pray in the middle of an ice cream store? And who but a freak would risk getting busted for her religious beliefs?" And then he smiled—that face-altering grin that revealed big straight teeth, white as Chiclets. "I happen to think freaks are kind of cool. Non-freaks bore me."

I didn't know whether to smile back or toss the rest of my drink in his face. But somehow it wasn't the kind of confusion that sent barbed wire coursing through my veins.

"So—are you a freak about anything?" I said.

He grinned even bigger. "I haven't found my freak focus yet," he said. "But I'm working on it. That's why I like to hang out with freaks. See what they're up to."

"Is that why you came up here?" I said.

"Yeah," he said. "That—and I wanted to see if you were really talking to a seagull."

"Yes, I was," I said.

"What did you say to him?"

"I think it was a girl. I told her she didn't know a good thing when she had it."

"Who does until they lose it?" Duck said. "You want an order of fries?"

I said yes. I broke my own antiguy vow for a container of greasy potatoes and the chance to talk to a boy who wasn't attacking me or laughing at me.

He's a person, I told myself. *Not a date.*

It doesn't matter that he's a person with shoulders like a wrestler.

We got into a conversation about where to get the best French fries in town, which somehow led to a discussion about how he wanted to be a diver rather than a swimmer—only Coach Powell wasn't a diving coach—and from there we went into my stalled singing dream.

"You'll get it going," Duck said to me. "As soon as you get over the laryngitis. What's up with your voice anyway?"

"I talk too much," I said. I pretended to ponder a fry. "The thing is, becoming a singer is only going to happen when and if God wants it to happen."

I let my glance slant over to him, and I watched him scan the horizon with sun-squinty eyes. He didn't say anything, but he didn't flinch either.

And then he nodded.

My cheeks went a deep shade of Laura-you-are-such-a-manipulator.

Okay, okay, God. So I did that on purpose to test him. I'm sorry—my bad.

At least I hadn't prayed over the fries. Not that they were worth giving thanks for.

"Okay, so these didn't make the cut," I said, tapping the now empty container.

"Next time, Wendy's," Duck said. "They're great if you dunk them in a Frosty."

"No," I said, "It's all about the curly fries at Jack in the Box. With ranch dressing."

"You want to put money on it?" His eyes were now squinting at me, twinkling blue. "No, we'll bet for time." Duck leaned forward until a silver medal nosed its way out of his shirt and dangled over his knees. "If you agree that Wendy's fries make the cut, I'll take you to Jack in the Box. Whoever wins there has to pick the next place. Deal?"

"Sure," I said.

Okay, so what else could I say to shoulders like that? And to a guy who talked to me like I was a human being—even if it was about fast food?

When I climbed into my car—and then raced home to change for rehearsal—I felt like something had just happened that was totally out of my control.

"He wouldn't fit into the slot I'd created for him, God," I croaked into the rearview mirror. "So now I have to find out where he DOES fit, right?"

No! I screamed in my head. *No guys!*

I was almost convinced by the time I wheeled into the driveway. If I was going to the prom for Celeste and Stevie's sakes, it was going to be with some guy I could correctly peg as a poser or a loser or SOME-THING—somebody I wouldn't be tempted to go out with ever again.

Duck wasn't fitting any of those descriptions.

Neither was Ponytail Boy—but I sure could have used him just then.

chapternine

But since Ponytail Boy didn't show up at that moment, and his Secret Admirer side didn't answer my note, I had to try to keep Duck Boy from swimming into my thoughts every other minute.

So that night after rehearsal, I e-mailed everybody on the pledge list, told them what had happened at school, and asked for prayers and suggestions. Doing that and falling asleep while I was breathing in God kept my mind off Duck.

But before school the next day he showed up at my locker, even ahead of the BFFs.

"How did you know where I'd be?" I said. I dropped down to fumble with my lock before he could see how red my cheeks were turning. But he squatted beside me, probably so he could read my lips. My voice was so gone, I had avoided my mother completely that morning just so she wouldn't drag me to the emergency room.

"You don't think I noticed you before?" he said. "I told you—you impressed me at the hospital thing way back when. After that I just, like, started seeing you everywhere."

I didn't mention that I'd never laid eyes on HIM before that day at the sub shop.

Dude, I thought. *Has he been stalking me?*

It would have been creepy-weird if he hadn't suddenly gone scarlet. It was hard to tell who blushed faster or brighter—him or me.

"So," I said, "What's that medal around your neck?"

He felt for his chest and turned redder, if that were possible. He was now ahead of me on the embarrassment meter, which meant I could pull my books out of my locker without dropping them on our toes.

"It's got a cross on it," he said. "It was my grandfather's. He was a minister."

"For real?" I said.

"No, he was one of those fake ones." Duck squinted at me, eyes twinkling. "Yeah, he was for real. I used to sit on his lap and play with this thing, so my grandmother gave it to me when he died."

"Hey, Duffy!" Celeste's familiar voice was shouting from ten lockers down. It stopped in midsyllable when she saw us hunkered down together. "Oh—sorry, kids," she said. She was shamelessly eyeing me with "I told you so" practically written in freckles across her nose. "I knew you two would be good together."

We're not together! I wanted to shout at her.

"Look, I don't want to interrupt anything," she said. "So let me just tell Duffy this one thing."

"No problem," Duck said.

Like we needed his permission. I gave Celeste a pointed look, which she ignored.

"Mrs. I. is back in school—I just saw her," she said. "She told me we're meeting today."

Before I could even ask for details, she beat a less-than-subtle retreat, winking at Duck as she went.

"She kills me," Duck said. And then he ran his hand over his hair and said, "I'll walk you to English."

Okay—he knew my schedule. That WAS freaky-weird.

But for most of the morning my mind was on Mrs. I.—except during history when Mr. Beecher refused to call on me or Stevie whenever we raised our hands. So much for extra credit points. Jeremy—who had ceased to stand for reason and sanity—was racking up most of them now, when he wasn't casting lustful glances at Allison.

When the bell rang for activity period, I don't know how many members of the student body I plowed down to get to Mrs. I.'s office. The whole way I just kept praying, *Please let her have worked out all the stuff. Please let her be Mrs. I. again.*

Evidently God had other plans. She was hauling everything out of a desk drawer when I got there, and my heart stopped.

"Where are you going?" I said. "You're not leaving?"

She looked up at me, her skin pinched between her eyebrows.

"Honey, I'm not going anywhere. What on earth would make you think that?"

I nodded toward the dead pens and unfolded paper clips strewn across her desk.

"I'm throwing away junk that's been accumulating in here since I got hired."

"How long ago was that?" said K.J. She let her bag drop to the floor and kneeled on a chair.

"Seven years ago."

"So why now?" I said.

Stevie was suddenly there putting her arm around my shoulders. "My mother cleans out drawers when she's stressed. When she starts alphabetizing the spices, break out the tranquilizers."

Mrs. I. tried to smile again, and then she sank back in her chair and ran her hand across her forehead. Several rubber bands she'd obviously pulled from the drawer were still wrapped around her fingers.

"All right—dish, Miz I.," Celeste said. "You got somethin' goin' on, and it's freakin' us out."

Joy Beth gave a grunt of agreement as she approached from the doorway. We were all there, huddled around our mentor, and when Mrs. I. looked up at us, her face was a tangle of emotions that tied me right into a knot again.

"It's all ridiculous," Mrs. I. said. "And I know it's going to blow over."

"Yeah, but in the meantime it's rippin' you up." Celeste perched herself on the edge of the desk. "How are we supposed to be empowered when we see you flounderin' around?"

"We all flounder from time to time," Mrs. I. said. "I just—" Her eyes closed for a moment. "It does affect you." She appeared to be measuring out her words in teaspoons. "All right—I'll tell you what I can, what you need to know."

We all leaned in. She looked at each of us in turn as she talked.

"The administration has requested that I allow one of them to sit in on all of our Group meetings."

"No stinkin' way!" Celeste said.

"That's what I told them—basically," Mrs. Isaacsen said. "Their next suggestion was that I leave the door open during our sessions." She held up a hand to keep Celeste from standing up on the desk. "I said no to that, too."

"But why would they want us to do that?" I said.

"They want to be sure I'm not proselytizing in here."

"What is UP with that word?" Celeste said.

"Mr. Wylie said the same thing to us after that demonstration," Stevie said to Mrs. I. "But we weren't doing that—and neither are you."

"That's exactly what I told them—on both counts."

"Mr. Wylie talked to you about us?" I said.

"He holds me responsible for the 'scene' you created out there."

"There was no stinkin' scene!" Celeste said. She popped off the desk like it was burning her behind. "If he wants to see a scene, we'll give him one!"

"No, you won't." Mrs. Isaacsen's voice was low and solid. The look she gave Celeste matched it.

"No, we won't," I said. "That's not what the pledge says."

Celeste turned on me. "I don't see what good the pledge has done us so far. Do you know how much trouble Stevie has had trying to get 50 lousy signatures? And she just told me how Mr. Blowhard has practically put a muzzle on you two in history class." She took a long-overdue breath. "We tried to follow the pledge and be all mature with Mr. Wylie. But he still told you, Duffy—YOU—that you had a reputation for making trouble! This is just messed up."

She was breathing like a John Deere tractor by that time and staring me down.

"Is the administration going to make you do whatever they say regarding our Group?" Stevie said.

Mrs. Isaacsen shook her head. "But they've given me a warning. If there is any evidence that I *am* trying to convert students to Christianity on campus, I'll be in violation of the law, and they'll have to take disciplinary action."

"Disciplinary . . ." Celeste said slowly. "You mean—you could get fired?"

"I don't think it will come to that—"

"But it's a possibility—"

"Let's not get all worked up over something that probably won't even happen—"

"But it COULD—"

"Celeste, stop!" I said. I had both hands to my temples. "Mrs. I., what do you want *us* to do?"

I wanted her to say we should pray. I was dying for her to tell us that would make the whole thing go away.

But she let her gaze turn to K.J., and her face reflected the kind of pain that had to come from deep inside of her. K.J. was the only one of us who didn't call herself a Christian yet.

"We shouldn't give anybody any reason to think you're breaking the rules," Stevie said. "We won't even bring up God when we're meeting in here."

Mrs. Isaacsen closed her eyes again like she was attempting to wrestle away the tears that were already dangerously close to the surface. I knew because I could feel mine staging their own fight. When she looked up again, it was at me. Every line in her face was screaming, *I don't want to say this, Laura! I would rather die than have to say it!*

"Stevie is right," she said. "All I can say is you should use your resources to know what to do."

"But you can't tell us that the resource is God," Celeste said. "They probably have the office bugged." She raised her voice and pointed it toward the ceiling. "Can you hear me now?"

None of us had much to say during that meeting, even K.J. She followed us out to the courtyard at lunch and stood there while we sat down, her arms folded.

"Whatever you've got to say, just say it," Celeste said to her.

K.J. ran a finger down all the studs— from top to lobe—that were stuck through her ear cartilage. "It's your fault she's in trouble."

"WHAT?" Celeste said.

Joy Beth rose from the table. It took two of Trent's hands planted firmly on her shoulders to keep her on the bench.

"You're the ones always bringing up—" K.J. looked over both shoulders and lowered her tone. "God and all that."

"But she's not trying to convert us!" Stevie said. "We were already Christians!"

"Well, I wasn't," Celeste said. "And neither was Joy Beth—but it was Duffy who made believers out of us, not Mrs. I."

"Don't say that too loud," K.J. said. "Or Duffy'll get 'disciplinary action.'" She twisted her lips for a second. "See, that's the thing. I hate it that y'all can't talk about what you're into." Her eyes drifted to Celeste. "I'd probably be in some stupid foster home if it weren't for you guys doing the church thing."

"But if Mrs. I. gets busted for this," Trent said, "you WILL be in a foster home."

"Thank you, Trent," Stevie said stiffly.

But K.J. was nodding. "It's the truth," she said.

Suddenly, they were all looking at me. And I didn't have an answer.

"I'm gonna pray about it," I said. "We all should."

Celeste gave a grunt that outdid Joy Beth. "Just don't let anybody see you doing it here."

So I prayed all afternoon with my eyes open and my mouth closed. There wasn't much I could pray except *Help!*, which was probably why I actually heard the whisper in my mind while I made a halfhearted attempt to fill in the quiz Mr. Howitch had just handed out. It echoed Mrs. Isaacsen's last bit of advice. I'd just finally shut up long enough to hear it.

Use your resources.

Resources. Right. My resources were Mrs. Isaacsen and sometimes my Secret Admirer, who still hadn't gotten back to me. And it wasn't like I could hunt down Ponytail Boy. I didn't exactly have his e-mail address.

So who else WAS there? If I told my parents everything, they would want me to just back off. Besides, Dad was so tired at night that he was always in bed when I got home from rehearsal. And my mother would probably have me admitted to the hospital for a tonsillectomy just to keep me away from any more controversy.

The BFFs were all waiting for ME to come up with something, and I wasn't getting answers from anywhere.

It seemed so clear at the retreat, I thought. *It was going to be so easy.*

Sure it had been easy—when everybody in the room was a Christian and we were all jazzed about doing something noble. But even though I'd asked them for prayer support, I hadn't received so much as an e-mail from the other kids at church. I wondered if Pastor Ennis had.

Pastor Ennis.

Pastor Ennis?

I could just see his shiny head turning red to the roots of what little hair he had left when I told him what we were into. I'd probably end up calming HIM down.

But once I thought it, it wouldn't leave me alone. I was still telling myself I was nuts when I called the church on my cell phone after school. Pastor told me to come right over.

I had never actually been in his office before, and I was surprised by it. It was neat and sort of minimally furnished, but everything in there seemed to make a statement, from the two overstuffed armchairs covered in bright stripes—immediately bringing to mind Joseph's many-colored coat—to the set of wind chimes in the window, gently jingling ceramic fruits of the Spirit in the breeze. I sank into one of the chairs and let a couple of my face muscles relax.

"You sounded stressed on the phone," Pastor Ennis said as he folded himself into the other chair. "Of course, your case of the croaks might have something to do with that. You aren't still hoarse from the retreat, are you?"

"It's just a thing," I said.

He looked at me as if he were trying to gain access to my mind files for several seconds before he said, "I think we need to start with prayer."

It was several more seconds after I bowed my head that he breathed, more than said, "Father, please be a third party to our conversation. Remind us to listen to you. Help us to loosen our grip on the things that have brought us here and lift our open hands to your presence. In the name of your Son, amen."

The rest of my face gave in in spite of me. I let my head fall back against the back of the chair, and I just breathed.

"Good," Pastor Ennis said. "Now tell me what's happening."

I poured out the story and, as I'd predicted, Pastor's face—and head—went crimson all the way to the hair follicles. But it wasn't embarrassment that caused it. He was actually angry.

"Unconscionable," he said, eyes flashing. "Your administrators have twisted the law to cover themselves. And they haven't given YOUR rights a second thought."

My eyes popped a little. I wanted to say, *Okay—who are you and what have you done with my pastor?*

"Mr. Wylie—that's the principal—" I said. "He wouldn't even listen to us."

"Have you considered talking to him again? Now that he's had a chance to calm down?"

"You think?" I felt a small stirring of hope. "It does seem like if we could just get him to hear what we were actually saying, we might be able to make him see that Mrs. Isaacsen isn't doing anything wrong—and neither are we."

Pastor Ennis was nodding thoughtfully. "Do you want me to go with you?"

I knew I was staring, but I couldn't help it. This was SO not what I'd been expecting. I felt a little bad about that, like I'd never really looked close enough to see who he really was.

"Right now," I said, "I think I should try it alone—you know, so he doesn't think we're trying to bust him by bringing in a minister."

"That makes sense. How can I help you?"

I studied my knuckles for a minute. "The way it always worked with Mrs. I.," I said, "was she would give me some Scripture to study, and I'd get my help from there." I didn't like talking about Mrs. I. in the past tense, like she'd died or something.

"Mrs. Isaacsen sounds like a very wise woman," Pastor said. "I like the way she works."

He stretched across his desk and retrieved an NIV Bible. It seemed to fan right open to the page he wanted.

"Mark, chapter 13, verse 11," he said. "Jesus told the disciples not to worry about words, but just to say what was given to them—'For it is not you speaking, but the Holy Spirit.'" Pastor Ennis glanced up at me from the book.

I tried not to look disappointed, but that wasn't what I wanted to hear. I wanted a plan, for Pete's sake! He was as vague as the Secret Admirer with his wedding invitation. Mrs. I., on the other hand, would be giving me wedding imagery from the Bible right now because she was that connected with where I was.

Pastor Ennis wasn't Mrs. I., but he was all I had.

"Did Jesus ever use—like, wedding stuff when he was teaching?" I said.

Pastor Ennis ran his long fingers through his Bible and spread them across the page he stopped on, almost as if he were trying to absorb it through his fingertips.

"Matthew 25," he said. "Can you handle reading it out loud?"

I took the Bible from him.

"Start at verse one. And why don't you get comfortable? I think God has something for us here." He loosened his tie and rolled up his shirt-sleeves.

"I'm fine," I said. If I had been with Mrs. I., I'd have kicked off my sandals and curled up in the chair. I really missed her.

"Okay," I said.

At that time the kingdom of heaven will be like ten virgins who took their lamps and went out to meet the bridegroom. Five of them were foolish and five were wise. The foolish ones took their lamps but did not take any oil with them. The wise, however, took oil in jars along with their lamps. The bridegroom was a long time in coming, and they all became drowsy and fell asleep.

I looked up at Pastor Ennis and blinked. *And this tells me what?* I wanted to say to him.

"Read on," he said.

At midnight, the cry rang out: "Here's the bridegroom! Come out to meet him!" Then all the virgins woke up and trimmed their lamps. The foolish ones said to the wise, 'Give us some of your oil; our lamps are going out.

I stopped to let my throat stop hurting. This had been a bad idea, I decided. It had nothing whatsoever to do with the Mrs. I. situation, as far as I could tell.

But I read on.

No, they replied, there may not be enough for both us and you. Instead, go to those who sell oil and buy some for yourselves. But while they were on their way to buy the oil, the bridegroom arrived. The virgins who were ready went in with him to the wedding banquet. And the door was shut.

I looked up again. "I already know what happens," I said. "The stupid ones come back and knock on the door, but the bridegroom tells them to go away."

"He says he doesn't even know them," Pastor Ennis said. His eyes were drooping as if he'd just witnessed the whole thing himself. "Read that last line, verse 13."

Convinced that he had the entire gospel memorized, I scanned the page. "'Therefore keep watch,'" I read, "'because you do not know the day or the hour.'" I closed the Bible. "Isn't this about Jesus coming back and people not being ready because they don't know him?"

"Exactly," Pastor Ennis said. "We have to keep watch and be prepared."

"But that other passage said don't prepare—just let God give you the words."

"Which we can't do if we don't know him."

"The bridegroom is Jesus, right?"

"Right."

"I know him—so how come it isn't working?"

"Oh, it's working." Pastor Ennis crossed one foot excitedly over the other knee and jiggled it. "You're here—you're reading the Bible—you're praying. Now you have to be like one of the wise virgins. Virginal, meaning not under the influence of the world." Pastor's eyes softened. "I've seen you with the youth group. You're not of this world, Laura. That's why it hurts you so much to have to be in it, looking at all its ugliness."

Almost without realizing it, I tucked my feet up under me. "That means—what—I wait?"

"Yes!" he said. You'd have thought my "final answer" had just made me a millionaire. "You know Jesus has what you need to know. So you wait. But you don't do it without backup because you don't know how long it's going to take."

"Backup," I said slowly. "That's the oil." I frowned. "So the oil represents—what?"

"Anything that will allow you to see Jesus when he comes to you with the answers. Not literally see him—but see what he has to offer you in this situation."

"But what IS that?" I said.

"What things help you to see the Lord in your life?"

I counted them off on my fingers. "Belonging to a community of believers. Worshiping. Praying. Reading the Bible. Listening." I looked at him blankly. "I already do all that."

"Then keep doing it," he said. "Don't stop—don't let your oil supply run out. If you need anything else, God will provide it as long as you're paying attention."

I nodded slowly. "And nobody else can do it for me."

"Exactly." His entire face—and part of his head—was shining at me.

"But I still don't have to do it alone, right?" I said. "Other people can do it WITH me, yeah?"

"That's what God wants."

There was something hesitant in his voice.

"If it's what God wants, then that's what'll happen," I said. "Right?"

"Is that always the case? Don't you think he wants every kid in your school to know Christ?"

"Yes."

"And is that happening?"

"What are you saying?"

"I'm saying it's great when you have people walking the walk with you, but if they aren't there yet, you still won't be alone. The Lord is always beside you."

"Of course," I said.

Besides, that wasn't something I had to worry about. The BFFs would always be on the path with me. Our bond went deeper than the pledge. God was what bound us together, and that was where we'd stay.

chapterten

When I left the church, I actually felt like I was untangling. My mind was clearer than it had been in days. The barbed-wire feeling had almost disappeared.

We can do this, I kept thinking all through rehearsal and even as I was falling asleep that night. *We can do this.*

Too bad I was using the wrong pronoun.

The next day—Saturday—all of us piled into Stevie's father's Expedition and went down to Panama Beach, the actual Gulf of Mexico. Even Trent went with us; he didn't "do" swim trunks, so he'd compromised and worn a pair of shorts that came down to his calves.

Stevie had hardly hit the Hathaway Bridge over the Bay before Celeste started passing around the suntan lotion. Meanwhile, I was spelling out the idea of our all going to see Mr. Wylie—my voice all but disappearing again in the process.

"We can do this," I said. "I know we can make Mr. Wylie see that Mrs. I. isn't doing anything wrong—and neither are we."

I glanced behind me at the third seat where Joy Beth was applying lotion to the back of Trent's neck—the only place, besides his face, that was actually exposed to the sun. "We'll really need to look at the stuff you got from the Internet," I said to him. "You didn't happen to bring it with you, did you?"

Trent looked at me like I was something out of *Ripley's Believe It or Not*. The rest of the car fell silent, too.

"What?" I said. "We CAN do this. Pastor Ennis was the one who thought of it. You wouldn't believe how good he is one on one."

Joy Beth grunted at me.

"I can't do it," she said. "I already told you that. Coach Powell will can me."

"It isn't like we're going to stage a protest," I said. "Nobody even has to know we talked to Mr. Wylie. It's just a conversation."

Joy Beth looked dolefully at Trent, who, except for the thick coating of zinc oxide on his nose, was the spitting image of Eeyore from *Winnie the Pooh* at that point.

"Until we get suspended or something," he said. "I don't think Wylie's changed his mind about us."

"We're not going to get suspended if we're respectful and just give him the facts," I said. "And if Celeste doesn't insult him too much."

Trent just looked at Joy Beth.

"So—if she's not in, you're not in?" I said.

"You could do it," Joy Beth said to him. She shoved her hair behind her ears. "I won't get mad."

Trent shook his head. "I'll give you all the stuff I found on the Internet, but I'm not going back in his office. I'm too close to graduation." Then he pulled his tiny mouth into a decisive knob, and that was that.

I turned back around and leaned my arms on the console between Celeste and Stevie. Celeste was staring at the road ahead as if she were driving the vehicle.

"You're in, aren't you?" I said.

"You really think this is the right thing to do?" I could see a tiny, delicate line forming between Stevie's eyebrows, just above her sunglasses.

"It might be the right thing to do," Celeste said. "But is it gonna work?"

"It will if we listen to God," I said. "He'll give us the words. It's right there in the Bible. We can be the three wise virgins."

"Excuse me?"

I gave them a raspy explanation. Still they stayed quiet. The line on Stevie's forehead got deeper, and Celeste opened a bag of bagel chips.

"What's the deal?" I said. "We all made a promise to defend people who are the victims of hatred, no matter who it is. Who's done more for us than Mrs. I.?"

Celeste scowled into the bagel bag. "I don't get why Gigi and them have something against her. She's not even Gigi's counselor."

Stevie adjusted her sunglasses. "I think it's about me. Gigi knows I love Mrs. I."

"How would she know?" I said.

"Trust me—she knows everything about me," Stevie said. "I think she's using Mrs. I. to get to me. Y'all know she's evil—but you don't know her like I do. Don't forget she used to be one of my best friends." Stevie shuddered. "It makes me want to vurp."

Celeste turned to me. "Okay, you set it up with Mr. Wylie, Duffy," she said, "and we'll be there."

She pushed her sunglasses back up to the bridge of her nose but not before I saw the glitter in her eyes.

"We have to stay really calm when we talk to him," I said. "We have to pray first—a lot—and we have to listen to God to know what we're supposed to say."

"In other words, get psyched up," Celeste said.

"Yeah—like be sure we have plenty of oil."

Celeste nodded. "Speaking of which—are you guys done hoggin' the suntan lotion back there?"

I looked at Stevie. She seemed to be something less than psyched, but she nodded at me, too. The line stayed between her eyebrows.

We didn't talk about it the rest of the day. Celeste kept us too busy eating from the huge cooler she'd brought, and Stevie was preoccupied with slathering herself and everybody else with the proper SPF formula and telling us all to turn over at regular intervals. And Joy Beth and Trent, of course, were too caught up in each other.

This feels kind of weird, I thought as I ventured out into the Gulf by myself. *It's like they're with me—only they aren't.*

Something was missing, something that had always kept us bonded. Yeah, Stevie was waving to me from the beach, and Celeste sat up and waved with her, gesturing with the sandwich she'd made for me. Even Joy Beth and Trent took their eyes off each other long enough to give me a nod.

They loved me. I loved them like I'd never loved any friends before. The thought of it swelled up in my chest.

Yet ever since I'd brought up Mr. Wylie on the drive over, they'd inched away from me somehow. Celeste talked more—and louder—than usual about everything BUT the issue we were facing. Joy Beth hardly said anything at all. Trent looked away from me when my eyes caught his. Stevie seemed to be watching me as if I were very far away.

From out there in the water they looked like a cozy vignette on the sand, a picture of friendship—without me in it.

That's not true, is it, God? I thought. *They're with me, aren't they? With me in you?*

Joy Beth suddenly bounded up from the blanket and started to barrel toward me as if Trent had kept her out of the water long enough.

Maybe it's okay, I thought. *Maybe I'm just too sensitive.*

Still, I knew how Mrs. I. must have felt, wanting so much to share an important part of herself and having her longing held back by some lurking, invisible thing. If she was like me, she couldn't even name it.

I could only call it loneliness.

That was probably why when Duck called me after I got home and asked me to meet him at Wendy's that night to dip French fries into Frosties, I said I would be there.

He was already seated in a corner booth when I showed up, and he stood up as I went toward the table. His turned-up nose was red, like he'd been out in his Sunfish all day, and his eyes were wide open and sparkly. The white Chiclet teeth flashed in the grin he seemed to have been keeping just for me.

Don't do it, Duffy, I told myself. *Don't complicate your life. It's just French fries.*

When I got to him and tossed my purse on the chair, he stood there, gazing down at me with that little-boy expression that didn't match his swimmer's body. There was almost something sad in his eyes, although that flickered away when he grinned again.

"You got some sun today," he said. "You look good."

I wanted to say, *So do you.* But I grinned back and nodded toward the spread on the table.

"Did you get enough food?" I said.

"You can never have enough French fries and Frosties. Are you sure you never did this before?"

"Uh-huh."

He put a hand on the side of my face, fingers reaching softly into my hair. "You don't get out much, do you?"

I could hardly breathe. All I could think was, *Don't do it, Duffy! But he has those shoulders. Don't. Those eyes. That little-boy smile. Don't do it.*

But sitting there across the table from him—getting complicated instructions for just the right dipping technique, feeling him laughing into my eyes—I was warmed like I hadn't been by my friends all day.

Don't do it could barely be heard when Duck was FEEDING me chocolate Frosty.

"More?" he said, gliding the spoon toward me.

I shook my head. "Can we talk about something serious?"

"Absolutely. On a scale of one to five, how do the fries rate—with five being the best and zero being those ones at the Marina?"

I actually giggled. *Don't do it?* I almost couldn't help myself.

"Uh—four," I said.

"Four? You're killin' me!"

"I have to leave a margin for the Jack in the Box trial," I said.

He glanced at his watch.

"Not tonight!" I said.

"Next date." He squinted at me. "This IS a date, right?"

What was he DOING to me?

"Okay," I said, with what little voice I had left by that time. "Since this is a date, I want to tell you about something."

His whole face went soft and threatened to melt me like the Frosty that was now sitting forgotten between us.

"You okay?" he said.

No!

"I just have this thing on my mind," I said. "My friends and I—you know, the Jesus Freaks—are going to go back in and talk to Mr. Wylie about Mrs. Isaacsen getting in trouble for supposedly preaching in her office—which she isn't doing."

"Man, that takes guts," he said. "I wish I had that much nerve."

I couldn't help staring at him. "You're kidding, right?" I said.

"No."

"With those shoulders? I thought you weren't afraid of anything!"

"You're not going in there to take Mr. Wylie out—you're going to stand up for your beliefs." He shrugged the shoulders in question. "I don't even know what my beliefs are half the time."

The cross medal was swinging outside his T-shirt. I reached across and took it in my hand. I had to ask him, and then the decision not to fall for this guy would be easier to make.

"You don't believe in what this stands for?" I said.

Duck curled his fingers around mine, still on the medal.

"I wear it because my grandfather believed it—and I want to believe it."

"Why can't you?"

His face went blotchy as he stared down at our hands. "Some of it just doesn't make any sense to me. I have, like, too many doubts."

"Everybody has doubts," I said. "I take mine right TO God because he's the only one who can clear them up."

When Duck lifted his eyes to me, they were sad again, and he wasn't hiding it.

"You're too good for me," he said.

There it was. He was making the decision FOR me. How much easier could it be than that? The next sentence would be, *I want us to still be friends.*

I tried to pull my hand away, but he held on.

"I hope I'm not too much of a loser for you," he said. "We have a lot more French fries to test."

He kissed the knuckles of my captured hand and kept his hold on it. I really hoped he couldn't tell that he'd captured my heart along with it.

"I guess I can put up with you," I rasped at him. "As long as I can help you with your doubts."

He searched my face as if he were looking for a crack. It suddenly struck me that I wasn't the only one who had gone to Wendy's that night with a decision to make.

"Deal," he said and stuck a French fry into my mouth.

✳   ✳   ✳

When I woke up Sunday morning, I had absolutely no voice. Mom said that if I didn't stay in bed and get rid of this thing, I WAS going to the ear, nose, and throat doctor the next day. There was no way I could miss school. That would mean no rehearsal, either, which would take me right off the stage crew. Mr. Howitch was strict about tech week.

And missing school would also mean missing a chance to talk to Mr. Wylie. Celeste and Stevie were acting so funky about it, I wanted to do it before they found some reason not to go.

And, of course, I wanted to see Duck.

God, he feels like a you-thing. Somebody I can actually help to find his way to you. It doesn't get any better.

What I did do that day was check my e-mail. None of the other kids in our youth group had responded, but there was one from Trent. He'd attached a bunch of stuff about religion and schools.

I liked what I read. Basically, the First Amendment guaranteed freedom FROM the imposition of religion by the government, including public schools. But it also guaranteed freedom OF religious expression as long as it was student-organized, outside classroom hours, and not disruptive.

Yeah, baby. Good old Trent.

I wasn't sure whether it was the prayers, the feeling that we were finally armed with what we needed, or the downtime I gave my vocal cords; but the next morning I was able to talk like I wasn't a baritone.

After deeming my temperature normal, Mom let me go to school. As much as I wanted to get another glimpse of Duck and make sure the whole thing hadn't been a dream, I nailed Celeste and Stevie at the lockers before Duck could get there.

"Can we go to the office now?" I said.

Instead of answering, Stevie put her arms around my neck and held onto me.

"What's up?" I said.

"We're feeling like losers," Celeste said.

"Why?"

Steve unwrapped her arms. "Saturday we thought you were being maybe a little—"

"Militant," Celeste said.

"But then we were in church yesterday, and Pastor Ennis preached a sermon about the virgins and the lamp oil."

"Go figure," Celeste said.

"And we realized you're just being your usual wonderful self." Stevie put her forehead against mine for a second. "We're just not as centered on the Lord as you are—and we need to be."

"I told you I wanted to be like you when I grow up," Celeste said. "So—time to grow up."

I noticed at that point that she was dressed like Michelle—a black skirt, conservative black flats, and a snowy white blouse that, admittedly, fit her like a second skin—but the overall look was definitely "I am credible." She had her hair down, the top and sides pulled back in a clip. Mr. Wylie probably wouldn't even recognize her, which I was sure was the point.

"Show us how, Duffy," Stevie said to me.

They locked their arms in mine; and as the three of us headed for the main office, I gave them the capsule version of what Trent had sent to me.

We are good to go, I thought. But Mr. Wylie's secretary interrogated us so suspiciously, I found myself looking around for the naked light bulb and the one-way window. Finally and grudgingly, she put us in his calendar for the following week.

"Next WEEK?" Celeste said. "No stinkin' way!"

"It's the only opening he has," Miss Prim said. I actually didn't know her name, and at that point I didn't want to. What I did want to do was keep Celeste from getting thrown into detention for roughing up the gatekeeper. The outfit wasn't doing much for her.

"I know he's busy," I said, "but this is really important. Will you let us know if he has a cancellation?"

Miss Prim looked at me through her square, silver glasses. "The only way you're going to get in to see Mr. Wylie any sooner is to get yourselves into deep trouble. And I don't think you want to do that."

"No, ma'am," I said. And with my hand firmly clamped around Celeste's arm, I steered her out of the office.

"That was hypernoxious," Celeste said when we were back in the hall.

"We just have to wait," I said. "There's a reason why it's going to take that long. It'll give us time to pr—"

"SHHH!" Stevie said. "We know what you mean, Duff."

"Okay," I said. "It'll give us more time to get enough oil."

We spent the rest of the morning procuring the last ten signatures Stevie needed for her official nomination. Going to classes was like an annoying interruption. By lunchtime she had five more.

"Piece of cake," Celeste told her as all the BFFs headed for the courtyard. "We'll just—Duffy—Duck alert!"

I turned around in time to have a muscled arm land around my shoulders.

"Hey," he said. "Can I take you to lunch?"

"Jack in the Box?" I said.

"Nope—save that for tonight after you get out of rehearsal. I'm thinking the lawn for now."

Because I couldn't breathe again, I just smiled and nodded and then looked at my BFFs.

"Y'all come, too," I said.

Celeste was the first to break free from the unanimous shock the four of them were exhibiting and said, "Oh, no. We wouldn't want to interrupt anything."

Duck led me off. I glanced over my shoulder to see Celeste with her hand up to her ear, phone style, mouthing *CALL ME!* with exclamation points in her eyes.

I felt a little detached, leaving them behind at our table. But the rest of the week really made that okay.

Stevie was totally occupied during lunch, canvassing for signatures and slowly squeaking out the ones she needed. And Celeste followed her around like the Secret Service, while Joy Beth and Trent kept Gigi under surveillance. With Stevie to take care of I doubted any of the BFFs were thinking—or praying—much about our upcoming meeting with Mr. Wylie. That fell to me. I made myself refuse to spend every spare moment—like there were so many—with Duck. He made it easier by telling me he was going to be out of the town for the weekend.

Our Group kept meeting with Mrs. I. twice a week. She was there, in body anyway, but I got the feeling she wasn't hearing everything we were saying. Not that we were talking about anything important. K.J. kept letting out those exasperated sighs that could say more than a set of encyclopedias, and Joy Beth and Stevie were looking at me as if I was the new topic fairy. Celeste, of course, made hypernoxious jokes and offered to talk about her love life.

I prayed constantly, and finally it seemed to pay off.

On Friday morning Stevie received a notice during second-period homeroom that she had been approved to run for student body president. That meant no teachers had blackballed her. Her counselor had approved her—which was a no-brainer, seeing as how it was Mrs. I.—and she'd finally gotten enough students' signatures to show their faith in her.

It was okay with me that Stevie had barely gotten 60 names and, according to Celeste's inside information, Gigi had gotten over 200. We didn't, of course, share that information with Stevie.

"Once the campaign really starts," I told Celeste, "people are going to see how much more amazing Stevie is than Gigi."

"It's gonna be a slam dunk," Celeste said. "Especially since WE are the people who are going to show them. I'm having T-shirts made up for all the BFFs, and we have to wear them every day. They could get pretty rank, so I'm having two done for each of us. What color do you think—"

It did actually sound like fun, especially that Saturday night when we all got together at the Books-A-Million coffee shop and Celeste presented us with turquoise shirts with orange lettering, as well as buttons, fliers, and kazoos. She demonstrated for us how to play "Hail to the Chief." I could barely get a squeak out of mine. My voice was getting worse again.

"You don't think they're gonna start something, do you?" Trent muttered.

He glanced anxiously toward the area with the couch and the overstuffed chairs. Gigi, Fielding, and her usual crowd, which now included Jeremy and Allison, were lounging all over the furniture as if Books-a-Million was their private country club.

"No," Celeste said. "But don't you just know they're going to show up at school with T-shirts after they've seen ours?"

"No way," Stevie said. "Gigi wouldn't be caught dead in anything that didn't come from Abercrombie and Fitch. Now—Duffy—" She pulled back the curls like she meant business. "Enough about them. What is UP with you and Swimmer Boy?"

I'd already been through it with Celeste, and I hadn't been able to convince her that it wasn't time to plan a bridal shower. After all, Duck and I only ate lunch together every OTHER day since he worked for Coach Powell during lunch period on Tuesdays and Thursdays. We hardly ever talked on the phone because he had swim practice after school and I had rehearsal at night. And we only got to see each other after rehearsal for a half hour. It wasn't like we spent EVERY minute together. We hadn't even had a chance to have any really serious conversations about his doubts yet.

"How come you're not with him tonight?" Celeste said.

"He had to go somewhere with his parents. He isn't coming back 'til Monday afternoon."

Celeste wiggled her eyebrows. "Should be a nice homecoming."

I smacked her. Duck hadn't even tried to kiss me—but I definitely missed the way he played with my hair and my hands and locked me into hugs with those honkin' huge arms. And that look he gave me that made me stop breathing.

But nothing made me forget the meeting with Mr. Wylie. Monday at lunch I reminded Celeste and Stevie that it was going to happen the next day.

"I need to make a positive connection with him," Stevie said. She smoothed out the "Elect Stevie" T-shirt, which she'd made to look like it was a designer top. I made mine look like—well, a T-shirt.

"It's totally gonna be positive," Celeste said. She stretched out on the bench and put her head in my lap. "I know I already apologized, like, 13 times, but I'm sorry about what I said the other day—about the pledge not helping us. It's working, isn't it?"

"Are you comfortable?" said a female—authoritative—voice.

I saw a pair of Big Bird-sized feet wearing pumps next to the bench. Mrs. Underwood was standing over us, imperious as a queen. I all but shoved Celeste off my lap and was about to make excuses for her when Mrs. Underwood turned to Stevie.

"May I have a word with you, Stephanie?" she said.

"Yes, ma'am!" Stevie said, and they disappeared through the doors into the hall.

"Dude," Celeste said. "What do you think that's about?"

"Something bad," Trent said. "You didn't see the look on Underwood's face?"

"Maybe she's telling Stevie that Gigi has done something to get herself kicked out of the race," I said.

Celeste grinned. "That's what I'm talkin' about!"

Still we waited like a jury was going to come in and give a verdict. I felt even more anxious when lunch ended and Stevie still hadn't come back. I took her bag to the office, hoping maybe I'd get a glimpse of her, but Miss Prim took it over the counter and ordered me to go to class before I could even turn my eyes toward Mrs. Underwood's closed office door.

Between that and still not seeing Duck, I was a network of nothing but nerves the rest of the day. I was about to have a serious breakdown as I headed for my car when I heard Stevie calling to me across the parking lot.

She was so pale when she got to me, her lips looked blue. The hand that held onto mine was clammy and shivering.

"What HAPPENED?" I said. "Are you okay?"

Stevie shook her head, and for a minute I didn't think she was going to be able to speak at all. When she did, her voice was flat and thin.

"Mrs. Underwood said that even though I got approved, a couple of the faculty members wrote on my recommendation forms that they had reservations about my 'subversive' Christian activities."

"Subversive?" I said. My voice disappeared up into the high range. "That's so bogus!"

"She doesn't think so." Stevie was raking her hair. "She said the administration was going to keep an eye on me throughout the campaign, to make sure I'm not—"

"Let me guess," I said. "Proselytizing."

Stevie nodded miserably.

"Okay," I said. I grabbed her wrist and pulled her back toward the building. "I don't care—we're going to see Mrs. I. I know she'll help us with this."

And with Stevie in tow I headed toward the school.

chaptereleven

We actually spotted Mrs. I. crossing the faculty parking lot and broke into a run to get to her. I let Stevie tell her what had happened. Mrs. Isaacsen put down her bag and rubbed her eyes with both hands.

"I don't know what to do," Stevie said. "Do I have to go around saying I'm NOT a Christian just to get elected? I mean, it feels like they're just looking for a reason to cut me out of this."

Mrs. I. looked like she was going to cry and never stop.

"Nobody can hear you out here," I said, although I was starting to think Celeste wasn't that far off in believing they had Mrs. I. bugged.

"It isn't that." She delivered a sigh. "Now I've been told not to have my Bible out on my desk when students are in my office. Among other things." Mrs. I. looked sadly at Stevie. "All I can say to you is that we can only behave as Jesus would have us do. But according to the administration, I shouldn't even say that much."

She gazed at each of us for what seemed like a long time before she got into her car. Stevie and I were left to look helplessly at each other as we moved back toward the building.

"I have to go back in for a meeting with all the candidates and Mrs. Underwood," Stevie said.

"I'll be praying the whole time you're in there—"

"Don't."

I blinked. "Don't pray?"

"Don't talk about it, Laura." I saw her swallow hard. "I don't feel like I can even have a conversation about it on campus. Maybe I shouldn't—"

"Hang out with me," I finished for her. My contacts were starting to swim. "Is getting elected that important to you?"

"It's the only way to change things around here," Stevie said. "I can't do that if I don't get elected—and I won't even be allowed to run if I don't do what they say."

"But we have the law on our side!" I said. "I read the stuff Trent gave me. We're allowed to pray or talk about God anytime outside of classes."

"They'll find a way to twist it—just like Pastor Ennis told you. You can see what they're doing to Mrs. I."

I pretended I had something in my contacts and blinked into my palm.

"Laura—just try to understand, okay? I can't go talk to Mr. Wylie with you. I can't be a part of any of it. But that doesn't mean I don't still love the Lord—and you."

"It's okay," I said. "Do what you have to do. I'll still campaign for you."

But she shook her head.

"It might be better for me if you don't even wear the shirt," she said.

Then she turned around and retreated into the building.

I had needed Mrs. Isaacsen in the past but never as much as I did right then. But there was no way I could go to her. I was sobbing so hard, I had to pop both contacts out and feel my way to my car. Inside I put my forehead on the steering wheel and bawled until I could hardly catch my breath.

So much for everybody wanting to be like me. One of my best friends doesn't even want to be SEEN with me.

I didn't know how long I'd been sitting there when I heard a tap on the window. Mrs. I. peered in at me, her face so pinched that she looked ten years older.

I fumbled for the window switch and finally just opened the door. She squatted down and took both my hands in hers.

"Are you all right, honey?" she said.

"No."

"How can I help you?"

"You can't."

Her eyes went stormy. "All right, this has just gone too far. You want to meet me off campus?"

"Can we do that?"

"Yes, my dear, we can." She didn't look like she cared even if we WEREN'T supposed to. She was my Mrs. Isaacsen again.

"I want us to have tea together," I said.

"All right—meet me at Panama Java—downtown on Harrison, just a block from the pier. My treat. Maybe we'll have a goody, too, huh?"

I couldn't get there fast enough—once I put my contacts back in. I'd never been to Panama Java before, but I didn't have time to really check it out. I just noticed it was a dark, quiet place with a tile floor and the smell of coffee showed it was obviously far richer than anything they served at Books-A-Million.

Mrs. I. steered me to a table and called over to the counter, "Shontelle? Two Earl Greys, honey, with lemon."

"The chocolate tarts are fresh," the woman said.

"Give us two."

Mrs. I. situated herself in the chair next to me and fluffed out a napkin.

"You must come here a lot," I said.

"This is one of my havens. Talk to me, Laura."

"I'm ticked off that we have to sneak away and hide in here just to talk! And you know what else makes me mad?"

"Tell me."

"Stevie told me I can't campaign for her because if I do, she might not get elected. She can't even be seen with me. And it's the same with Joy Beth—she doesn't want to get kicked off the swim team because of me. So the only person left is Celeste. I hate this!"

"I hate it, too."

Somewhere in the midst of my tirade, the tea and tarts had arrived. When I didn't touch mine, Mrs. I. spooned honey into my cup and stirred.

"I wish there was a way I could tell you this is all going to be okay," she said. "But I can't. We can both pray in our hearts, live out our faith, and witness by example—but sometimes that isn't enough."

A shadow passed over her face, and it chilled me.

"I have to tell you something," she said. "I just feel like you ought to know."

I didn't want to hear it, but I nodded anyway.

"At the end of this school year I think I'll probably leave Panama Beach High."

"No!" I said. And then I crunched down on my lip. "I'm sorry. That's kind of selfish of me."

"Not at all. And don't you think it makes me happy to know that I've helped you?"

"You've saved me! And not just me—"

Mrs. I. put a clammy palm over my hand. "That's just it. It's getting harder and harder not to bring God into it when I see how some of the kids are suffering when they come into my office. But I never have—except with people who bring God in with them—like you, Celeste, Joy Beth, and Stevie."

"And now you can't even do that."

"And yet it's what I'm called to do," she said. Her eyes were moist again, making her eyelashes clump into little bunches. "If I can't answer God's call here, I have to go elsewhere. They have an opening at Cove Christian."

I wanted to scream NO again, but I pulled myself back from it and stared into my tea. Neither of us was eating the chocolate tarts.

"I'll serve out my contract for the year," she went on, "but I'll have to do what I can to keep from getting fired in the meantime. That doesn't look so good on a resume."

She tried to smile, but she failed. I finally took a sip of the lukewarm Earl Grey so she could get control of her trembling mouth without me staring at her, begging her not to fold.

"Laura," she said. "You'll be okay without me. You've come so far."

"I don't feel like it. I feel like I have to cut everything off from God when I'm at school so I don't hurt Joy Beth or Stevie—or you."

Mrs. I. shook her head sharply. "You do what you think is right. Just don't do it in anger." She took my fist in her hands and gently uncurled my fingers.

"I don't even know what IS right anymore," I said. "It seemed so easy with my friends beside me—and you. Now I just feel like I botch up everything I try to do for God."

"Don't be so hard on yourself. This is a tough situation."

My shoulders sagged. "I feel bad for even telling you all this, with all you have to deal with."

"That's what Christian sisters do for each other. You want a little advice?"

"Ya think?" I said.

"The people who are giving you and me and Stevie a hard time—they can't judge us."

"Only God can."

"And do you know how he does that?"

She motioned to Shontelle for more hot water.

"He stands us up next to Jesus," Mrs. I. said, "and he looks to see if we're like him."

I tried to get an image while Mrs. I. poured hot water over my tea bag in a fresh cup.

"So it's kind of like that thing at the eye doctor," I said. "They put up that slide with two circles and they say, 'Tell me when they come together.'"

"Into one circle," Mrs. Isaacsen said.

I frowned into the steam coming up from my mug. "If I'm close to him, then he's the ONLY one I'm close to. I'm so lonely right now."

"What about your boyfriend?"

I almost knocked the cup over. "Boyfriend?"

"I was about to leave after I talked to you and Stevie today when some young man came along and said you needed my help in the student parking lot. I assumed he was your beau."

"Tall guy with big shoulders? Short, reddish hair?"

My heart was suddenly beating faster.

"No," Mrs. Isaacsen said. "This one was very slender—and ooh, the eyes. You don't often see eyes like that on a young guy. I've never seen him before—I don't think he's a student."

I didn't dare ask if he had a ponytail. And Mrs. I. didn't ask if I thought he was my Secret Admirer—whom we'd talked about so many times back when we could actually bring up stuff like that in her office.

So Ponytail Boy WAS around. Even as elusive as he was, it was comforting.

"I know one thing for sure," Mrs. I. said. "God is going to give you opportunities to defend your faith and unite his children. Just wait and be ready."

That was what Pastor Ennis had said. Goose bumps pimpled my arms.

We left without eating the tarts, but I still wasn't hungry. So I got together as strong a voice as I could muster and called Mom to tell her I wasn't coming home before rehearsal. Then I headed back to school, thinking I could camp out in the green room and get some homework done.

When I pulled into the parking lot, I was surprised to see Celeste's Mercedes still there.

That's weird, I thought. Celeste never hung around the school any longer than she had to—unless it was to talk to some guy she found momentarily fascinating. In that case she was probably holding court on the side lawn.

And as I rounded the building, I discovered she was there, all right. Only it wasn't the boy *du jour* she was talking to. It was Gigi Palmer.

chapter twelve

It definitely didn't look like Gigi and Celeste were comparing prom dress notes. Gigi was drawn up to her full five foot nine; but even though she was bearing down on Celeste, my friend had her face right up in Gigi's as if she were examining her dental work. I couldn't hear what they were saying, but the faraway muffle of their voices reminded me of that conversation I'd overheard on the other side of Mrs. I.'s door.

Celeste is going to get herself in SO much trouble if she loses it, I thought, and I shot across the yard with my backpack pounding against my spine. I was about 30 feet from them when somebody stepped right into my path and put his hands on my shoulders. The way I stopped, which involved stumbling forward and falling right into his chest, it wasn't hard to see that it was Duck. Up close and personal.

"Hey you," he said.

I felt like I was being torn in half. Behind him Gigi and Celeste were still going at it verbally, and I had to stop them. But then there HE was, smiling down at me with that look in his eyes.

"Hi, Duck, nice to see you," he said.

I blinked and tried to focus on his face. "It IS nice to see you. I just—"

"Your voice is getting worse," he said. "You've gotta go to the doctor. You want me to take you?"

"No—Duck, I need to talk to Celeste. Didn't you see her—"

"Who?"

"Celeste! The girl who introduced us! She's over there about to—"

Duck pulled me into his chest with one hand behind my head. "Did somebody introduce us?" he said in a voice not much louder than mine. "I feel like I've always known you."

I momentarily forgot the impending catfight.

He held me out to look at me, his hands still on my arms. "I've been thinking about a lot of stuff over the weekend, and I want to talk to you about some things."

"Okay," I said. "Like what?"

"Not here." He took my hand like he was about to lead me away.

"I have rehearsal," I said. "And I need to find out what's going on with—"

"Meet me after," he said. "And in the meantime—just think about this." He pulled me close again, up into his face. "Think about going to prom with me. That's not the only thing I want to talk to you about—but just think about that first."

I didn't have a millisecond to even start. From across the lawn I heard Celeste's voice slashing the air. The words were clear this time.

"Nothing you say can hurt us, Gigi!" she shouted—into Gigi's nostrils. "So why don't you knock off the harassment?"

Gigi's voice was no less loud and no more controlled. "You and your little friends are the ones doing the harassing—and we CAN hurt you—in a MAJOR way."

I wrenched myself away from Duck and tore over there. By the time I got to Celeste's elbow, Gigi was waving a piece of paper—which I snatched out of her hand.

"Give me that!" she screamed, this time at me.

I only had a second to look at it before she ripped it away from me.

"What is that?" I said. "It looks like a petition."

"Well, aren't you just the valedictorian?" she said. Her glossy lips were curled into their usual sneer. There was something very sure and triumphant about it.

"A petition for what?" Celeste said. She made a grab for it, but Gigi was too fast for her and dangled it over her head, out of Celeste's reach.

I was tall enough to snatch it back again, but this time I turned away from her so I could read it. Just before she managed to reach over my shoulder and pluck it up, I saw the words *that Mrs. Isaacsen be removed.*

That wasn't all I saw. There must have been 500 signatures at the bottom of the page.

"You really think that's going to get Mrs. Isaacsen fired?" I said.

"No stinkin' way!" Celeste lunged for the paper again, but Gigi quickly stuffed it into her bag.

"If we could get rid of a teacher just by signing a petition," I said, "there wouldn't be a faculty member left in this school."

"It isn't just the signatures," Gigi said through her nose. The hair flipped over her shoulder. "It's what she's done."

"What did she supposedly do?" Celeste said. She was matching Gigi sneer for sneer. I'd always known Celeste had it in her; I'd just never seen it before. She wasn't our sunny little beach bunny at the moment.

"You really think I'm going to tell you so you can run to her and she can start covering it up?" Gigi laughed. It was the most purely ugly sound I'd ever heard.

"You witch!" Celeste said.

She threw herself at Gigi, fingernails bared, and I had to put both arms around her from behind to keep her from clawing Gigi's face. Not that I wouldn't have relished the sight of that.

"Don't bother, Celeste!" I said, though I was sure she couldn't hear me over her hissing and spitting. "It doesn't mean anything because it isn't true."

"It'll mean something when the school board gets ahold of it," Gigi said. "And that's where it's headed."

"You TRAMP!" Celeste cried.

I wasn't sure I was going to be able to hold her back for much longer. She was wrestling against my arms like somebody straight out of WWE.

"Go away, Gigi!" I shouted hoarsely. "Just leave!"

"I'm not afraid of her!"

"You should be!" Celeste pulled up her wrists and got them under my forearms, giving a heave that would have put Joy Beth to shame.

I was sure my arms were broken, but I was still clawing out to get hold of her again when somebody stepped in and shoved the two of them apart. Mr. Howitch used his stocky arms to hold them at bay while BOTH of them flailed and shouted obscenities. Let's just say that Celeste was no longer stringing benign words together.

Then someone else appeared and pulled Celeste back. Duck was too strong for her to get away from HIM.

"Knock it off, both of you!" Mr. Howitch said.

Celeste went slack against Duck. Gigi was still pummeling the air.

"Gigi—I mean it," Mr. Howitch said. "You can't afford to get a detention."

I actually wished she'd keep on fighting. If she got busted, it would solve a lot of our problems.

But Gigi dropped her arms and stepped back, giving Celeste a look meant to rip out her cheekbones.

"Now both of you," Mr. Howitch said, "get as far away from here as you can—and in opposite directions."

Gigi dug her heels in until Celeste glared up at Duck, who let her go. She retrieved her bag and stomped off toward the parking lot.

"Celeste!" I said. I started after her, but Duck stepped in front of me again.

"You okay?" he said.

"Yeah—where were YOU?" I said.

He put up both hands. "I don't get in the middle of girl fights. Good way to get your eyes scratched out."

"No kidding."

I glanced over my shoulder. Gigi had already disappeared; Mr. Howitch was making his way back into the building, shaking his head.

I snapped myself in the other direction, but Celeste was already climbing into her car. I was pretty sure I couldn't calm her down. I'd never seen her that way before.

"Hello? Duffy?"

I looked at Duck.

"I said—why don't I meet you after rehearsal, and we'll finish what we were talking about?"

I took one last look at Celeste's car as it peeled out of the lot, and then I nodded at him.

"You okay?" he said.

"I don't know. " I said it into his chest as he pulled me in.

"You will be," he said. I felt him kiss the top of my head before he let me go.

✳   ✳   ✳

I didn't know which feeling to land on as I set up for the first act. K.J. worked that out for me when she showed up and asked me to help her with her costume.

"Don't you have a dresser?" I whispered to her as we headed for the dressing rooms.

"I don't want her," she said over her shoulder. "I need you."

It didn't feel like a compliment. K.J.'s eyes were so narrow, I couldn't see her pupils.

She slammed the dressing room door shut behind us and didn't reach for her Puritan garb. When I did, she grabbed my wrist.

"Mrs. I. got a phone call just when I was waiting for my ride. It was from the superintendent's office."

"Superintendent—"

"Of Panama Beach School District. Mr. Big Man. The one who hires and fires."

"What was it about?" I said. I had to lean against the counter, or I was going to fold to the floor.

"I don't know. That's all she would tell me." K.J. ripped off her shirt, revealing her braless state. She snatched her costume off the hanger herself.

There was a tap on the door, followed by, "You need some help, K.J.?"

"Go away!" K.J. said.

She waited until the footsteps receded before she lit into me again, her back turned toward me so I could button her up. "Deidre was out there honking her horn in the driveway, and I was standing there trying to figure out whether to leave or go back and find out why Mrs. I. was in her bedroom crying like a baby."

I closed my eyes. I could see Mrs. I. curled up in a fetal position, her head buried in a pillow. It was one of the scarier thoughts I'd ever let myself have.

"Something big is going down," K.J. said as she turned to me again. Her face was pale, accenting dark shadows under her eyes. "We gotta find out what it is and stop it."

"We? Do you think you should help?" I said. "What about the play?"

"I'll find out something, and I'll tell you—but nobody can know I'm involved."

"Five minutes!" Benjamin yelled through the door.

"I have to go," I said. "Eve'll be having a coronary."

"If you want to take me home after rehearsal, we can talk about it," K.J. said. She suddenly looked small—and frightened.

"Okay," I said, and then I stopped. *Duck. Rats!*

"I can't," I said. "I promised I'd meet somebody. I could try to call him—"

"Nah—don't worry about it," K.J. said. She was visibly retreating back into her contained self. "We'll talk tomorrow."

"I'm really sorry—about everything," I said.

"You started it, Duffy," she said. "You're the one who has to end it."

Through the whole rehearsal even Eve was more on the ball than I was. Afterward I thanked her several times for saving me from making a complete fool of myself in front of the entire cast and crew.

"I didn't do anything!" she said. But she was beaming—even her bangs were like golden spikes poking out from her scarf. "I'm just glad to see that you make mistakes, too. I thought you were perfect."

You have no idea, kid, I thought. But maybe I would feel better when I talked to Duck. After the way he held me that afternoon, I felt like I could tell him anything.

I sure didn't have anybody else at the moment.

By the time I got outside, a lot of the cast and crew had already left. I stood under one of the lights and surveyed the parking lot for Duck.

I spotted his shoulders right away—like I could have missed them—and I was about to head for them—him—when I realized he was deep in conversation with somebody.

That somebody was Gigi.

I was rooted to the sidewalk.

Gigi?

Duck told me he didn't know her. On the day of the demonstration when he'd supposedly chucked Gigi's sign and left, he later told me he didn't even know her name.

But as I watched them with my heart frozen in my chest, I could see that this wasn't a chance encounter with an acquaintance. He was standing there with his hands in his pockets, but his shoulders were bulging, as if he were half mad and half defensive. Whenever she paused, he thrust his head forward and spewed out something from a mouth so tight I could practically hear it creaking when he opened it. Maybe it was my imagination, but I thought I could see his eyes flashing from 50 feet away.

I was now grateful for those 50 feet between us because they gave me the distance I needed to back up toward the building and slip inside without either one of them looking my way.

Go to your locker, Duffy, I told myself as I stalked through the lobby and into the hallway. *Get away from everybody so you can think.*

Like I could KEEP from thinking. The thoughts were slamming together inside my head by the time I got my hands on my lock.

What is going on?

What's he doing with Gigi?

Why does she have to take absolutely everything away from me?

And what about the petition? Does he know about that?

Has the whole thing with him been just lies?

I yanked the locker door open, and a parchment envelope fell out. Right behind it was a tiny glass object, which I managed to grab before it smashed to the floor.

My mind was so scrambled, I had to stare at it for a full ten seconds before I realized it was a miniature oil lamp, perfect in every detail—right down to the cloth wick. The only thing missing was the oil.

I ripped open the envelope and unfolded the note. My hands were shaking so hard you'd have thought I was a drug addict.

You are being prepared to be one, it said in that perfect handwriting I had come to know so well. *Stay awake, for you must find something you need.*

"Oil," I said out loud.

And then I leaned against the locker and banged my fists into it.

"Would somebody PLEASE give me a straight answer?" I shouted.

But nobody said a word. Not even God.

chapterthirteen

When I got back to the theater lobby, Mr. Howitch was locking the doors. He pulled on his nose when he saw me. He was well into worry mode.

"You ARE still here," he said. "I almost locked you in."

"Sorry," I said. "I had to go to my locker."

"So did you stand up your date on purpose—or was that just temporary insanity?"

His eyes darted nervously toward the door.

"My date?" I said. "Oh."

"He was asking for you. He looked a little ticked off even before I told him you'd already gone. I really didn't know you were still here."

And it was obvious Mr. Howitch wasn't happy that I was. The way he kept glancing at the exit, he definitely had someplace else to be.

"It's okay," I said. "I'm out of here."

I went for the door, expecting him to beat a hasty retreat behind me. But he stopped me with a firm, "Laura."

I turned to see him give his nose a hard tug.

"You're going to hear some things tomorrow that aren't true," he said.

"About what?"

"Mrs. Isaacsen."

My insides collapsed like an accordion losing air.

"Is she getting fired?" I said. I knew it was ridiculous. Gigi couldn't possibly have gotten to the school board with her bogus petition already.

But Mr. Howitch didn't deny it.

"I've said more than I should as it is," he said. "Just—whatever you hear tomorrow—if it's negative about Mrs. Isaacsen, don't believe it. You've got to keep your faith in her."

"I will!" I said. "But what—"

"I'm telling you what I already told K.J.—stay as far away from this mess as you can. Please." He nodded his head sadly toward the door. "Come on—I'll watch you until you get in your car."

I might have felt more alone in my life than I did on my drive home, but I couldn't name when. I even made up my mind to talk to my father about it, but he'd already gone to bed by the time I got there. Mom was still up, though, pretending she hadn't just been pacing the kitchen.

"Sorry I'm late," I said. "I was talking to Mr. Howitch."

She put her arms around me and hung on. "I know I worry too much," she said. "And Celeste sounded so strange on the phone."

"Celeste!" I pulled away from her.

"She's called about six times." Mom tapped an apple-bordered piece of paper on the table. "I kept telling her you were at rehearsal, but I guess she thought there would be some miracle and Mr. Howitch would let you out early."

I glanced at the kitchen clock. It was already 9:30.

"She said to call her no matter how late it is," Mom said. "I think you should—she really sounded stressed."

I bet she did! I thought. *And she's going to get worse when she hears from me.*

I kissed Mom's forehead and grabbed the portable phone on the way to my room. Celeste answered in the middle of the first ring.

"Where have you BEEN, Duffy?" she said.

I didn't explain. I didn't have a chance.

"Did you SEE what was written on Gigi's petition?" she said.

"Yeah, some of it—"

"They're trying to get rid of Mrs. I. They can't do that, can they?"

"I don't think—"

"I can't be responsible for what I'll do if something happens because of all this, Duffy. I swear, I'll take out every person between here and—"

"You can't, Celeste!" I was gripping the phone so hard I was surprised I didn't draw blood.

"What am I supposed to do—sit around and pray? This calls for action—we have to fight fire with fire!"

"No!" I said. "We have to stand up for Mrs. I., but we can't lower ourselves to their level."

There was a stiff silence.

"You're talking about that pledge, aren't you?" Celeste said.

"That" pledge. Not "our pledge." Not even "the pledge." THAT pledge—the one she was already distancing herself from so she could point at it.

"I'm talking about God," I said. "He doesn't want us to scratch Gigi's eyes out—what was that about this afternoon?"

"It was about me being sick of sitting around and doing nothing."

"So we'll go in and talk to Mr. Wylie tomorrow. We'll camp out at his door until he lets us in."

"Right. Then he'll write us up and stick us in detention while Gigi goes out and gets Mrs. I. canned." The sarcasm was so thick I was choking on it.

"God will give us the right words to say to change Wylie's mind," I said. "Pastor Ennis said it. The BIBLE says it. Mrs. I. even said it. I haven't even had a chance to tell you that I got to talk to her today—"

I stopped. Celeste's silence was screaming over me.

"Don't get me wrong, Duffy," she said finally. "I still believe in God. But I'm pretty ticked at him right now. Let's just say I'm not speaking to him." I could hear the phone being shifted to her other ear. "Where was he when we tried to stand up for him that day during the demonstration? Where was he when Wylie was yelling at us? Where was he when they started putting Mrs. I. down? I sure didn't see him this afternoon when Gigi was about to rip my ear off!"

"He was there," I said stubbornly.

"Yeah, well, he's going to have to speak up a little, or I'm not listening."

"You don't mean that!" I said.

"Don't tell me what I do and don't mean! We've got enough people telling us how to think and what to say and what to do. I'm done."

"Done with what?" I said.

"Done with this whole do-it-God's-way thing. If God wants me to do something a certain way, he'd better just tell me—loud and clear—'cause I'm sick of waiting. Meanwhile, I'm gonna do what I have to do."

"What does THAT mean?"

"I don't know."

"Celeste, please don't do something stupid," I said.

She gave a hard laugh, one that sounded more like Gigi than my best friend. "I don't think I'm the one who's being stupid right now," she said.

And then she hung up.

Is it necessary for me to say that I didn't close an eye that night? But even through my sleep-deprived fog the next day, I heard every piece of verbal trash Mr. Howitch had predicted.

My history class was the worst, with Allison spearheading most of it. Everybody ignored the assignment on the board so they could whisper and pass notes littered with stuff like—*Mrs. Isaacsen molested a kid.*

Mrs. Isaacsen molested ten kids.

Mrs. Isaacsen molested Mr. Howitch.

I would have laughed, except people were actually gobbling up that dog food. Even Jeremy—Mr. Fact—was swallowing it whole and vurping it back out to anyone who would listen to him.

I didn't know if Stevie was hearing any of it. She was the only student in the room who was burying herself in the textbook, not looking at anybody. Including me.

By lunchtime the courtyard was abuzz with rumors like, *Mrs. Isaacsen holds kids hostage in her office until they agree to get religion.* And *This whole Jesus thing is a hoax so she can lure kids into her office for who knows what?*

I didn't have any trouble hearing it because I was eating by myself. Fortunately, it was a Coach Powell day for Duck; I couldn't handle seeing him yet.

"Where are your friends?" Eve was watching me out of her wide blue eyes, swimming in worry.

"They're all busy with other stuff," I said.

"Want to sit with me and Holly?" She nodded toward the frail little thing seated next to her who always looked like she was about to take flight. Even her hair, flipped up all over her head, made her look airborne.

It was a little pathetic that a junior would have to accept the pity invitation of a freshman, but it beat sitting there pretending like I was perfectly content in my state of rejection.

"Sure," I said.

I parked myself at their table—and then I was at a loss for a conversation topic. I hadn't felt this way since I'd been the new kid my first two weeks at 'Nama High.

"Is something the matter?" Eve said. Her baby face was earnest. "You look a little freaked out—I mean, not in a bad way—maybe you aren't freaked out—I don't even know you that well, but it just seems like—"

"I'm fine," I said. "I just have a lot on my mind."

Holly actually whimpered. I must have looked pretty scary at that point.

But Eve was unscathed. "That's a bummer," she said. "Is there anything I can do to help?"

"No," I said. And then a thought grabbed me and shook me. Without even glancing over my shoulder, I said, "Do you pray?"

"Me?" she said. She looked at Holly. "I guess so."

"Then just pray that the truth will come out," I said.

"Okay," Eve said. The way she was blinking at me, I figured she was the only person at 'Nama who hadn't heard the rumors yet.

They didn't stop, not even in music theory class. I discovered the artsy types could really be creative with a good piece of gossip.

Somebody said, "Mrs. Isaacsen embezzled all the money that the Odyssey of the Mind team earned to go to state."

"No," somebody else said, "she's lobbying to get mandatory prayer back into the public schools. She's prepared to go all the way to the Supreme Court!"

And then there was the embroidered version of that: "She's threatening to expose Mr. Wylie's deep, dark secret if he tries to stand in her way." What the secret was they hadn't dreamed up yet, but I had no doubt it would be something especially juicy.

I tried not to listen to any of it, like Mr. Howitch had said, but since nobody could seem to talk about anything else, it was hard not to hear it. I definitely didn't believe any of it; he didn't have to tell me that. But what I couldn't do was stay away from "the mess." After school I marched straight to the office. Miss Prim was away from her desk, and there was Mr. Wylie, just about to go through his door. I pounced.

"Mr. Wylie," I said. "I need to talk to you—now."

He turned and eyed me out of his Doberman face.

"Please—I know you're busy—but this is important."

"It always is," he said.

His voice was weary, and for the first time I noticed that his eyes had a tired look. It made me feel a little better, not seeing victory oozing from every pore.

"So what's on your mind, Miss Duffy?" he said as he fell heavily onto the fake leather couch across from me.

"What people are saying about Mrs. Isaacsen," I said. "None of it's true."

He didn't say anything.

"If she's in trouble, it's because of me. I spoke up against Gigi at that demonstration, but Mrs. Isaacsen never told me to do that. And she never talked to any of us about Christianity if there was someone in the room who wasn't a believer."

He looked like he was about to say something, and then he crimped his lips together.

"We need her here, Mr. Wylie," I said. My voice was sounding desperate—and loud all of a sudden. "Please don't let the school board fire her."

"I have no control over that," Mr. Wylie said.

"Can't you tell them they're wrong—that what was on that stupid petition is just lies?"

I could see him forcing an understanding smile onto his face.

"Let me just reassure you that whatever happens will be based on the facts," he said. "You don't need to worry about it."

"But I AM worried about it! Mrs. Isaacsen is the best thing that ever happened to me. I wouldn't HAVE Jesus in my life if it wasn't for her—I'd be lost!"

Those may have been words from God—they probably were—but the minute they were out of my mouth, I knew they weren't the words that were going to get Mrs. Isaacsen out of trouble.

"But she didn't convert me!" I said quickly. "I was already a Christian when I met her! I just asked her questions, and she helped me—but not in front of anybody else. Sometimes it wasn't even on campus!"

Mr. Wylie rubbed his paws together as if he were wiping off my every word. "Fine," he said. "I'll keep that in mind."

"Are you sure?" I said. "You have to believe me!"

"You've spoken your piece, Miss Duffy. I've heard you."

He stood up and held out an arm as if he were going to guide me to the door like the perfect gentleman. I cringed inside and out.

"I said I heard you," he said. "I'll do what's fair in this situation. That's what I always do."

I shot up from the chair, clenching the sides of my skirt in my fists. "Do you?" I said. "I didn't think you were very fair that day you brought us all in here—"

"That's enough," he said. He was starting to growl. "Do you want me to put you in detention with your friend Miss Mancini?"

I froze. "Celeste got a detention? Why?"

He cocked an eyebrow, a sure sign he didn't believe that I didn't already know.

"Fighting," he said. "Somebody said something to her that she didn't like, and she jumped the boy."

"A boy?" I said.

"It doesn't matter who it was." Mr. Wylie drew himself up, stretching his neck to escape his shortness. "Make no mistake—I'll suspend you, too, if you continue to disrespect me."

It was all I could do not to poke him in the nose.

"I said I will be fair," he said. "There are things about this that you don't know and don't need to know. Leave it to the administration to handle it."

I didn't answer as I stalked toward the door.

"I mean it, Laura," he said.

As I forced myself not to slam the door behind me, the only thought in my mind was how ugly my name sounded coming out of his mouth.

I wanted to go to Mrs. I. Instead I called Pastor Ennis.

He said he'd be right over.

chapterfourteen

I wasn't sure what we were going to do once Pastor Ennis arrived, but HE knew.

"We're going to see Mr. Wylie," he said when I met him at the front entrance of the school.

His face was grim, and he had Miss Prim rapping on the principal's door in about two seconds. With Pastor standing beside me, being so sure of himself, I definitely felt less like a rabbit jumping back into a foxhole. But that was also the thing that had my teeth chattering.

What if Mr. Wylie gets MORE ticked off because I dragged a minister in here? I thought.

All I could do was pray. I couldn't even hope to get to my peaceful place right now. I just silently screamed.

Mr. Wylie didn't look quite so much like a trained attack dog this time. He smiled at Pastor Ennis and shook his hand before offering him a place to sit on one of the couches. Me he all but ignored.

"I understand you met with Laura already this afternoon," Pastor Ennis said. He looked from me to Mr. Wylie until the man had to acknowledge my presence with a nod.

"She doesn't feel she had the opportunity to say what she needed to say," Pastor went on. "I'm here to be sure she gets that chance."

"I heard everything," Mr. Wylie said. "And I told her I would keep it in mind."

Pastor leaned forward over his thighs. "You might want to talk to HER. I'm just the third party witness."

Mr. Wylie had no choice but to look at me again. This time there was a threat lurking behind the resentful expression on his face.

But I straightened my spine and looked right back at him.

"I was a little out of control when I was in your office before," I said. "I'd been hearing ridiculous rumors about Mrs. Isaccsen all day, and I was afraid you believed them. I'm sorry about that."

If Mr. Wylie nodded, I missed it.

"It just seems to me," I said, "that people don't understand Mrs. Isaacsen. She isn't proselytizing. She just lives a Christ-centered life, and most of the time she does that without saying a word."

"Most of the time?" Mr. Wylie said. I could have sworn his ears went up into Doberman points.

"The only time she talks about it is with those of us who are AL-READY Christians. I know the law. She's allowed to do that."

Mr. Wylie smiled at me, but in the way a kindergarten teacher smiles when a five-year-old says something cute. I was sure that small gesture was for Pastor Ennis's benefit alone.

"You're right," he said, "but that isn't what this is about."

"So what IS it about?" I said.

He pulled back, the smile frozen in place. "I am not at liberty to discuss that with you. Nor do you need to know. What I'm asking you to do is trust me."

I turned to Pastor Ennis. His jaw muscles were twitching.

"There's the issue, sir," he said. He looked down at me. "You're not certain you CAN trust him—isn't that it, Laura?"

"Right," I said. I honed in on Mr. Wylie again. His smile had melted into a line. "And that isn't disrespect. That comes from the way you talked to us that day after the demonstration. You said I'm a troublemaker. I don't think it's making trouble to stand up for the truth."

Mr. Wylie folded his arms across his chest, which was looking smaller by the minute compared to Pastor Ennis.

"What can I say to convince you that I will be completely fair?" he said.

"Respect our rights," I said. "SCHOOL-sponsored religious activities are prohibited by the constitution, but STUDENT-sponsored religious activities are protected by the constitution under free speech."

"I know the law—"

"But I think you've been more concerned about being politically correct," Pastor Ennis said. "I certainly don't envy the position you're in, but I believe you have an obligation to protect everyone's rights." He pulled a folded piece of paper out of his pocket. "This is a copy of a letter sent to every public school principal by the American Center for Law and Justice, just in case you didn't get yours. It explains the free speech rights of students in more detail."

"I'll certainly read it," Mr. Wylie said. "But let me make it clear that what I am concerned with are TEACHERS overstepping their rights, not students."

He suddenly smiled cheerily, as if it were time to break out the refreshments. "Anything else I can help you with?"

✳ ✳ ✳

I was so distracted at rehearsal that night, Eve had to tell me what to do.

And it wasn't just the meeting with Mr. Wylie that had me chewing on the ends of my braids. I was also concerned about the two official-looking women who came in during our intermission break and pulled K.J. into a corner of the green room. It drove me up the wall during the whole next scene—but I didn't have to wait long to find out what was going on. The minute she came offstage for the last time, K.J. grabbed my arm in a vicious grip and dragged me into the stairwell.

"You know who those two chicks were?" she hissed. "They were from Social Services."

"Not good," I said.

K.J.'s eyes were narrowed, snake-like, striking right at mine. "They told me that if Mrs. I. gets fired, I'm going to be put into a foster home—unless I want to go back to my dad."

She didn't have to add that she would rather live with a family of Bengal tigers.

"I don't think she's going to get fired, K.J.," I said. "She hasn't done anything wrong."

"What difference does that make? Somebody's out to get her. And you—" She poked her index finger hard against my sternum. "You have to find out who it is and stop them. I already told you that if I find out anything, I'll tell you—and you better use it."

I couldn't say a word. What does a person say when she has pure hatred staring her in the face?

"Are you going to sit around and pray about it?" she said. "Or are you going to DO something?"

"I'll do whatever God tells me," I said.

She hissed again, a derisive sound that rendered God useless, at least to her.

"You just better be listening then," she said. "Mrs. I. has a hearing on MONDAY."

"Do you know what it's about?" I said.

"Like anybody's gonna tell me," K.J. said.

And as she walked away, I knew she was going to hate me for the rest of my life if I didn't start fixing things. She and everybody else I cared about.

I never did do my postshow tasks. I just sat on the stairs and sobbed—completely unaware of anything going on around me. At one point Deirdre stopped and quizzed me from what felt like several miles away. And Eve put her arms around me and rocked me until I told her to please leave me alone.

The only person who got my attention was Mr. Howitch, long after the cast and crew had vacated.

"Do you think you can drive, Laura?" he said.

I didn't, but I nodded anyway.

"Okay—I'm going to follow you home. You and I need to have a talk—and I want your parents there to hear it."

At home Mom took one look at me, got Dad out of bed, and put on a pot of coffee. The mugs stood untouched as Mr. Howitch told us everything.

"When Gigi Palmer returned to school after her suspension, she was still suspended from activities, but the administration also made her go see Mrs. Isaacsen twice a week to try to find out the root cause of her hatefulness."

"It didn't do any good," I said.

"Gigi made it seem like it did. She snowed Mrs. Isaacsen like a New England blizzard, trying to convince her that she was reformed." Mr. Howitch smiled wryly. "You know our Mrs. I. She saw right through that, and she advised the faculty and the administration to keep an eye on Gigi. She, of course, did the same."

I was having a hard time imagining Gigi in Mrs. I.'s office. I was pretty sure they hadn't shared Earl Grey.

"It wasn't long," Mr. Howitch said, "before one of the teachers suspected that Gigi was trying to intimidate some poor child into dropping out of cheerleading tryouts just so someone from Gigi's group would have a better chance of being chosen for the team."

"She needs to come up with some new material," Mom said. "They were doing that when I was in high school."

"The teacher couldn't prove it, but Mrs. Isaacsen told Gigi that if it turned out to be the truth, she was going to blackball her if she tried to run for student body president." Mr. Howitch looked at my parents. "Any teacher can do that."

"Thank heaven," Dad said.

"But she didn't get the proof," I said. "Gigi's running against Stevie."

Mom shook her head. "Now that's just not right."

"This is where it gets ugly," Mr. Howitch said. "Gigi looked for a way to get back at her. And Mrs. Isaacsen's Group—you girls—became the perfect target."

"Because that would take down me and Stevie and Celeste and Joy Beth, too."

"And Trent. Don't forget how he was essential in getting her friends convicted for what they did to you."

Dad was looking more pinched by the second. He squeezed the bridge of his nose between his fingers. "I take it the mess didn't stop there."

"No. The initial results weren't good enough. Gigi got to run for president, but so did Stevie."

"She'll win, won't she?" Mom said. You would have thought Stevie was her kid. I didn't have the heart to tell her that Stevie and I were barely friends now.

"Gigi took matters into her own hands and evidently got some student to say that Mrs. Isaacsen had threatened the kid with eternal fire if they didn't get down on their hands and knees right there in her office and come to Jesus."

"That didn't happen!" I said. "Don't they see it was all Gigi?"

"That's the problem. It's impossible to link this student to Gigi, and it's basically the kid's word against Mrs. I.'s. And then at the demonstration, when you—one of Mrs. I.'s prize pupils—stirred things up, the administration thought they had reason to doubt Mrs. Isaacsen."

"But it didn't have anything to do with her!" I said. "That was all me—and I tried to tell Mr. Wylie that—and so did Pastor Ennis."

My parents both looked at me as if I were speaking in tongues. I realized, guiltily, that there was a lot I hadn't told them.

"My heart breaks for her," Mr. Howitch said.

"Can't you do something?" I said.

He ran his finger back and forth under his nose. "I'm supporting her. I'm quashing rumors in the faculty lounge, much as I hate going into that den of iniquity. I've been to see Mr. Wylie and the superintendent—but I don't have anything more solid than the fact that I know Mrs. Isaacsen and can't see her doing something like that."

"I'm going to make some calls myself," Dad said.

Mom picked up the coffeepot and made a move to warm up their cups, but nobody had even taken a sip.

At least now I knew what was going on. But that only took me so far. I needed the name of the kid who was doing this to Mrs. I. Mr. Howitch had been careful not to even reveal whether the little liar was a boy or a girl.

And there was no way I was asking him. He'd already told me more than he should have, I knew that. In fact, I didn't even feel like I could tell K.J. what he'd said to us. Not K.J. or any of the BFFs. Even if it meant they'd never help me unless I did.

I'm alone in this, aren't I, God? I thought later as I climbed into bed. There was no answer, and I couldn't keep my eyes open to wait for one.

All night I kept dreaming that someone was whispering the word *One* to me.

chapterfifteen

I had to drag myself out of bed the next morning. Even before I got my eyes all the way open, Duck came to mind.

I brushed my teeth with a vengeance. He'd lied to me—that was obvious. And now, knowing what I did about Gigi and the kid who was accusing Mrs. I., nothing he had ever said to me rang true. Nothing.

For a hopeful second I toyed with the idea that he and Gigi had just met that very minute when I saw them fighting, and he'd instantly seen her for what she was and got on her case.

But I couldn't buy that story. I had to face the fact that he was working for her—and that all the attention he had shown me was just a part of her scam.

I knew I should have kept my vow and stayed away from boys, I thought. *I get burned every time.*

Maybe seeing him fighting with Gigi was a God-thing, though, and in more ways than one. As I pulled on a pair of capris, it struck me—if Duck knew about Gigi's plan, he could be pretty useful to me. I could use him while he still thought he was using me.

I yanked on a T-shirt and shook out my hair, pretending I was shaking him off me. Then I stood up straight and looked at my bedraggled self in the mirror. I had to find out what he knew, and the only way to do that was to get back into his good graces.

"EWWW!" I said to my face in the mirror. "Talk about hypernoxious."

Celeste would probably have the perfect manufactured word for this situation. I missed her so much. She could have helped me with the plan that was formulating in my mind. Now I was going to have to find somebody else.

Duck didn't meet me at my locker again before school, which was no surprise. It actually hurt more that nobody else did either, except Eve. I looked behind her as she bounced up to me, her bangs feathering, but she was Holly-less.

"Where's your friend?" I said.

Eve shrugged. "We're not hanging out anymore."

"There's a lot of that going on. Did you guys have a fight?"

I looked into my locker with studied nonchalance, but there was nothing from the Secret Admirer. A little help—even in the form of a riddle—would have been a nice touch about then.

"We didn't really fight," Eve said. "We just aren't into the same things anymore."

"That happens," I said.

I stood up and closed my locker with my foot. As I did, the proverbial light bulb seemed to appear over my head.

"Would you deliver a note for me?" I said to Eve.

Everything on her bounced, including the jumble of charms on her watchband.

"Yes!" she said.

"Okay, see that guy with the big shoulders—"

She scanned the crowd, and her eyes darted back to me as if the mere sight of Duck had stunned her.

"You don't mean THAT guy?" she said. "In the swim team T-shirt?"

"Yeah," I said. I peered closely at her face as it seemed to pale at the very thought. "Is that a problem? Do you know him?"

"No!" she said. She looked completely flustered. "It's just—he's so cute!"

"Yeah, well, he's mine," I forced myself to say. It was like hearing somebody else talking with my mouth.

"I wasn't going to try to steal him from you!"

"Just keep an eye on him while I write this. Then take it to him."

Eve obediently scoped out Duck while I opened my locker again and yanked a piece of paper from one of my binders. It was scary how much influence I had over this little freshman. I just wished I weren't using it this way.

But I have to, I told myself firmly. *It's for Mrs. I. It's for all of us.*

"He's getting away!" Eve hissed to me.

I scratched out a note: *Meet me at lunch, okay? I want to explain about last night.*

"Here," I said as I tucked it into Eve's hand. "I owe you."

I was sure she didn't hear that. She was already going after Duck like she was about to make a tackle.

I watched her until Duck was actually reading the note, then I abruptly squatted down to my locker just before he looked up to search for me. That was when I saw what I'd missed before—a neat parchment envelope hidden under the binders, along with a tiny blue vial.

Please don't confuse me more than I already am, I thought as I slit the envelope open and read the note: *Prepare to greet your bridegroom in humility. You will be as One.*

Let me guess, I thought as I held the blue bottle up to the light. *This is oil.*

What had the story in the Bible said? The wise virgins had enough oil to last them until the bridegroom came. I looked doubtfully at the little one-ounce bottle. This would last me ten minutes anyway.

I put the vial back in my locker and closed it. It was a good thing I was on automatic pilot as far as my schedule was concerned because as I went on down the hall, my thoughts had nothing to do with where my English classroom was located.

In the Bible the bridegroom was Jesus. I needed to be prepared for him—somehow. The Secret Admirer always spoke in symbols. If he didn't literally mean oil, what did he mean? Something for a lamp—something to see by. Something to help me see when Jesus was coming to—maybe rescue me—and Mrs. I.—and all of us?

I have to find whatever it is SOON, God, I prayed silently, *because we need you NOW.*

I gave a Joy Beth grunt. Duck was a far cry from Jesus, as far as I was concerned. But if he helped me clear Mrs. Isaacsen—it had to be a God-thing.

It had to be.

Which didn't mean I wasn't a basket case by the time the lunch bell rang and I stood outside the courtyard in the hall. Duck hadn't sent me a note back, and I hadn't seen Eve to find out what his reaction had been. Chances were he wasn't even going to show up.

But he was suddenly there with that hunchy, blotchy, embarrassed look that I hadn't seen in a while. His eyes were round and wary, and he ran his hand over the top of his hair and licked his lips—he did everything but hold up a sign that said,

I AM SO NERVOUS I COULD HURL!

"Can we just go sit in my car?" he said.

I only felt a small pang of guilt as I took advantage of his current neurosis.

"Then you aren't ticked off at me," I said.

His eyes widened. "I thought you were mad at ME."

"Something just came up last night," I said—in that other person's voice.

He let out a long breath, but he didn't actually seem relieved. As I followed him out to the parking lot and climbed into his green Honda Civic, I was halfway convinced that the case of nerves that made him chew dried skin from his lips was for real, that he was actually nervous that I was trying to dump him.

I can't feel sorry for him, I told myself firmly. *It isn't about him and me anymore.*

The sad thing was, it never had been.

"So," I said when he finally climbed in beside me. "Are you okay?"

"No," he said. "I didn't know why you stood me up. I thought maybe I scared you off by asking you to the prom. I thought we—"

"Sure, I'll go with you," I said.

Slowly, he grinned at me, that little-boy smile I USED to think I was falling in love with. The word *vurp* came sadly to mind, but I swallowed that—and my better judgment—and smiled back at him.

"So—are you hearing the same rumors I'm hearing about Mrs. Isaacsen?" I said.

He took my hand and twirled my class ring on my finger. "I've heard people talking about her," he said. "Who is she?"

I watched the side of his face for clues, but he wasn't a jaw twitcher like some guys.

"She's a counselor," I said. "THE counselor."

"Oh. I have Mr. Bloomfield. Weird guy. He plays with his eyebrows when he's talking to you."

"Nuh-uh!" I said.

Duck gave me a tentative grin. "I'm serious. I think HE needs a therapist."

"Ya think?"

The grin got bigger. "You're cute when you get sarcastic like that," he said.

I wasn't feeling terribly cute.

"I better get to class," I said.

"I'll walk you," he said.

"No, that's okay. I need to run and see somebody."

"Some guy?" he said.

I stopped halfway out the door. He was actually getting green around the gills again.

"No," I said. "You're my prom date, right?"

And then I fled, from myself as much as from him.

I headed straight for the guidance counseling suite, where Michelle was sitting at the secretary's desk, algebra book open, staring into space.

"You okay?" I said.

"Fine," she said. She nodded toward Mrs. I.'s door, which currently bore a sign reading,

MRS. ISAACSEN IS OUT OF THE OFFICE TODAY.

"I'd be better if she were here."

That took me away from the Duck issue for a minute.

"She always has the answer, doesn't she?" I said.

Michelle shrugged. "There IS no answer for me this time."

I set my backpack carefully on the floor. "What's happening?"

She looked up at me, her black eyes guarded, as always. Even as I watched, though, the shields fell.

"She can't stop my mama from dying," she said.

I put my hand over my mouth.

"She's been dying for a long time. Only it's worse now—they say it won't be that long. That's why I had to give up activities. I don't have time for them, with sitting with her."

"I'm so sorry," I said.

Michelle stared at the sign on Mrs. I.'s door. "She just makes it not seem so bad. And now they're all over her with this stupid—"

"It's okay," I said. "I already know."

She nodded. "I hear things in here. I know it's not true, but there's nothing I can do—about anything."

"Maybe there is," I said.

She cocked an eyebrow.

"It isn't illegal or anything. I just need to know who Neil Duckwell's counselor is. It could help Mrs. I."

Michelle didn't even hesitate. She flipped open a binder on the desk and scanned its contents.

"He's out of luck if he wants to get in to see her," she said. "It's Mrs. Isaacsen."

I barely saw her close the binder, hardly heard her say she'd already been in to talk to Mr. Wylie to tell him that Mrs. I. never tried to talk to her about the Bible. I'm not sure I even said good-bye.

chaptersixteen

There was no doubt about it now. Duck had lied to me—and about things he didn't even HAVE to lie about, like the name of his counselor.

I knew there was only one reason he would do that, and that was to keep me from suspecting he had anything to do with the Mrs. I. situation. He obviously had no idea I already knew, and I thanked God that I had seen him with Gigi. I'd been ready to tell all that night. I had been ready to trust him.

It wasn't a big leap from there to my next thought: *What if Duck made those accusations against Mrs. I.?*

Mr. Howitch had said it was somebody the administration couldn't trace back to Gigi, and Duck was trying pretty hard to distance himself from her.

Besides that, he was a good actor.

He ought to be in this play, I thought later that night while I was sweeping the stage before rehearsal. I moved the broom back and forth so hard I could have peeled the paint right off the floor.

He could get a Tony Award.

After all, I had bought his performance, hadn't I?

I told myself I was an idiot for having that kicked-in-the-stomach feeling. It was my own fault. I'd known better than to fall for a guy—

ANY guy. Not even Ponytail Boy, who wasn't helping me at all with his oil and his lamps and his wedding invitation.

But if trying to hold back a throat full of tears made me an idiot, then I was a certified case. That was probably why, as I watched K.J.'s last scene from the wings, I couldn't keep them back any longer.

K.J.'s character, Mary Warren, was being pulled in half over a decision she had to make. On one side she was devoted to John Proctor and to God, but on the other side she was afraid of her BFFs who were asking her to live a lie that was ultimately sending people to their deaths. And if she didn't lie, then she herself would be hanged as a witch.

The guy playing John Proctor, who had long ago ceased to be a normal high school senior to the rest of us, took K.J.'s—Mary Warren's—face in his hands and told her to do what was good and right. But the power of her friends was too much for her—they accused her of turning into a bird and coming down to tear their faces. In the midst of the pandemonium, even as John Proctor held onto the weeping Mary Warren to keep her from being torn from the arms of God, she wrenched herself away from him, threw herself into the midst of the scheming girls, and screamed at him not to touch her because he was the devil's man.

In the wings, with tears pouring down my face, I clutched at a curtain so I wouldn't run onto the stage and yank Mary Warren to her senses. It wasn't K.J. out there anymore—it was every kid who was torn between God and a dark world.

She was Joy Beth.

She was Celeste.

She was Stevie.

Maybe she was even Duck.

She was definitely me.

I was still crying when I drove home that night. *I can't give in like Mary Warren did,* I told myself. *I have to stay on the God side.*

But staying there seemed to mean that I had to hang between the two worlds until I found out what I needed to know, and it was tearing me up inside.

"Is it safe here, God?" I said.

I heard the whisper in my thoughts.

One.

"But what does that MEAN?"

I pulled into our driveway and sat there staring at my swollen-eyed self in the rearview mirror like I expected God to show up there and answer me outright.

One.

"What is with the ONE thing?"

I kept looking in the mirror, kept hearing the word over and over until I felt like I couldn't have another thought until I understood this one.

"Okay—okay," I said. "One."

I closed my eyes. Ones. I had to think of ones.

There was obviously only one person in the car right now—me. And it had been just me for what seemed like a long time now.

No, I thought. *This One has a capital letter. I can hear it.*

And I had seen it. My eyes came open. The Secret Admirer used a capital letter for it when he wrote it in my invitation—*Oneness will be celebrated. You are being prepared to be One. Prepare to meet your bridegroom. You will be as One.*

But that wasn't the only time. I had seen it and heard it someplace else—but when? I closed my eyes again, and the image of the eye doctor's circles coming together was right there.

When I heard the word *DUH!*, I was pretty sure it didn't come from God.

I had to be as much like Jesus as I could be—Mrs. Isaacsen had told me—so we would be like One.

The circles moved toward each other in my mind. I couldn't be One with anybody else. Not when there WASN'T anybody else. How much clearer could it be, for Pete's sake?

"Okay, God," I whispered in my pathetic little lost voice. "What am I doing that isn't like you?"

I was hanging in there when everybody else had run scared. That was a God-thing.

I was praying more than ever—and listening. I was good to go there.

And I was trying to find oil—I was doing everything I could to help Mrs. Isaacsen, using my resources like she said. I was doing it by—

Lying.

The circles stopped moving toward each other, and I squirmed under the seatbelt that was still fastened across my chest. Duck wasn't the only one who had been going for the Tony. Ever since I'd seen Gigi and him fighting that night, I had been putting on an act for him, letting him think I liked him so he would talk—maybe slip up and give me some information.

I did it for the right reasons, though, God!

But I couldn't even say it out loud, and he obviously wasn't going to accept that rationalization. Even the thought felt so un-Jesus-like, I wanted to vurp. Only one thing would bring my circle closer to his—I couldn't lie anymore.

"Then what AM I supposed to do?" I said.

One, came the whisper.

"So if I try to be like you, I'll know what to do?"

The whisper turned into a sigh that came out of my own chest.

✻ ✻ ✻

When I woke up the next morning, the sun was streaming into my bedroom, and the clock blinked a scandalous 8:30 at me.

I started to scramble out of bed when Mom poked her head in my door.

"Get dressed," she said. "We have a ten o'clock appointment."

Dr. Sutherland was a tiny woman with a chirpy little voice who took one look down my throat and switched to a tone that was less birdlike. "It isn't your throat," she said. "It's your vocal cords. I want you to see a voice specialist."

"How soon can we get in?" Mom said.

"We'll try to get an appointment ASAP." She frowned. "I see some growths on your cords—could be polyps, or cysts, or something else. In the meantime I'm going to give you a button to wear that says, 'I'm on voice rest'—and I don't want you to speak a word unless it's an emergency. We need to get that swelling down."

"No school then," Mom said to me. "You won't be able to stay quiet around Celeste and them."

"But—"

Dr. Sutherland got her face sternly close to mine.

"Are you a cheerleader?" she said.

"No," I said. "I'm a singer."

"If you want to sing again—period—you'll do exactly as I say. We'll give you a letter to take to your teachers." She flicked a glance at Mom. "Most teachers are happy to get this news."

I was glad I wasn't supposed to say a word because I was sure I would have screamed that she had to be out of her mind. I had things to say—important things—to Duck. I needed my voice.

But then there was the whisper—*One.*

I nodded at the doctor and crossed my heart.

They got me an appointment with the voice specialist for Monday. Mom said since there was only one school day between now and then, plus the play, it would be okay.

"Celeste will make sure you don't talk," she said.

I was glad I couldn't tell her that none of the BFFs were talking to me anyway. She looked sad enough already.

The only thing I could do for the rest of the day was listen and watch. The discoveries I made were very telling.

When I finally got to school, toward the end of lunch, I was at the counter in the main office signing in when I saw Holly—Eve's former flippy-haired friend—practically holding a press conference at the other end. She was regaling a bunch of freshmen girls with the tale that someone had planted a cross on Gigi's lawn the night before.

"Guess who?" she said in a sage voice that indicated they all KNEW already.

Interesting. Holly had always come across as kind of a wimp to me. She was definitely holding forth like a politician now. She was on somebody's payroll.

As I made my way to class, several people looked at my button and said, "How come you're on voice rest?" They didn't seem to get why I didn't answer them.

Eve caught up with me, and once she figured it out, she apparently didn't mind my silence. She happily chattered away and barely noticed that I wasn't chattering back. In the short walk to the science building I found out that she was an only child, she used to go to private school until this year, she wished she were taller—and she wished she were more like me.

I had to raise an eyebrow at that one, but she insisted.

"I always wanted somebody I could look up to," she said. "Older girls have always let me down before—but I know you're different." To my surprise she looked like she was about to cry. "I'll try not to let you down, I promise."

I was glad I couldn't answer her. I might have cried myself.

When I got to chemistry, everybody was talking about "those yellow fliers." Deidre planted one on my desk. GOD WILL GET ME ELECTED, it said.

Deirdre tapped Stevie's name at the bottom. "That wasn't very smart of her," she said.

I rolled my eyes. The fact that her last name was spelled wrong was more than enough to convince me that Stevie had absolutely nothing to do with it.

"Yeah, well, listen to this," Deirdre said, leaning into me like we were part of some conspiracy. "Somebody burned a cross on Gigi's lawn last night. You can only guess who did that."

It wasn't just a freshman rumor, then. In fact, it was all I heard about for the rest of the day, including after school when Gigi was in the locker area telling an adoring crowd that Stevie's people had started the rumor, but she was squelching it because she wanted to run a clean campaign.

Please.

I didn't catch the rest of it—not that I could have stomached it—because Duck was suddenly there, towering over me. Before he could hug me—VURP!—his eyes lit on my button.

"You finally went to the doctor," he said.

I nodded.

"Okay. We don't need to talk anyway."

The look that had once taken my breath away now came at me like a drooling leer. I fastened my eyes on a point above his shoulder. He turned around and seemed to assume I was glaring at Gigi.

"I don't even listen to that stuff," he said. "How can anyone believe what they hear from Gigi? She's always been a liar."

For the first time that day I had the urge to use my voice.

Always? I wanted to say. *You told me you barely knew her.*

"She's got that reputation," he said—too quickly. "She'll never get elected. You don't need to worry about Stevie."

It was such the perfect time to lay it all out and tell him that I knew he was a lying sack of cow manure. But I couldn't speak, and I had to be okay with that.

One, I told myself.

One, the Whisper said back to me.

"Look—" Duck's voice was suddenly soft and husky as he slipped his arm around me. "If you don't want to go to that cast party at the beach on Sunday, we don't have to. We can just hang out together. That way you won't be tempted to talk."

How did you know there's a cast party?

"I know you like to go to the beach—but we can go on our own. I still have things I want to talk to you about." He suddenly looked sheepish, as if he were about to make a confession. Just as quickly he covered it up with the smile that lit up his face. "At least now I'll be able to get a word in once in a while," he said.

I shook my head and opened my mouth. No matter what it did to my vocal cords, I had to say no to this date thing—I just couldn't do it anymore. But he tapped my button with his finger.

"I hope the show goes great tonight," he said. "I have some stuff I have to do, but I'll see you Sunday. I'll pick you up at noon."

I gaped after him as he disappeared down the hall. I was still shaking my head—but he hadn't even seen me.

chapterseventeen

The opening performance of *The Crucible* went so well that night, the audience gave a standing ovation. They must have clapped for ten minutes. Even Benjamin was grinning—and sweating like a faucet. I grabbed Eve and hugged her and jumped up and down with her flopping rag-doll style. I tried to just touch K.J. on the shoulder after the curtain call, but I could have been a speck of lint, the way she brushed me off.

Friday night's show also went well, but Saturday night's was even better. Mom and Dad went, and they both came out looking teary-eyed.

"You'll be up on that stage in the fall, honey," Mom said to me.

"Which is why we have to get this voice thing taken care of." Dad put his arm around me. "You can't catch a break, can you, baby girl?"

Eve ran up to us, her blue eyes looking soulful, and said, "You're coming to the cast party tomorrow, right?"

"Cast party?" Dad said to her.

Eve was, of course, happy to fill him and Mom in on the details. She was totally getting into her role as my mouthpiece.

"Do you have a ride?" Mom said to me.

I nodded. There was no way to get in touch with Duck to tell him not to pick me up—and it might be my only opportunity to tell him what I knew and get him to 'fess up before Mrs. I.'s hearing on Monday. How I was going to do that without talking, I had no idea. All I could depend on was God's oneness.

"So she can come?" Eve said.

When Dad said yes, she did some kind of cheerleader thing and practically turned cartwheels out the door.

"How can you say no to that?" Dad said.

"You're obviously her hero," Mom said to me. She kissed my nose. "You're mine, too."

✳   ✳   ✳

Although I prayed most of Saturday night and almost broke a sweat begging God during church on Sunday, I was still dreading going all the way to St. Andrew's State Park with Duck. If it weren't for Pastor Ennis, I might have chickened out completely.

"I think our youth group needs to meet again," he said to me when I was on my way out of the church. "It doesn't sound like things are going well with my little BFF core, and I'd like to see that healed."

Without Eve there my eyes had to do the talking for me. I could feel them bulging with a *How did you know?*

"I had Celeste change the plugs and points on my car yesterday," he said. "Let's just say some tears got mixed in with the oil."

When my own tears filmed my eyes, he said, "You have enough on you right now, Laura. Why don't you leave Celeste to me?"

✳   ✳   ✳

Thank heaven for prescription sunglasses. I cried so much between church and lunch, my eyes were practically swollen shut, and I couldn't wear my contacts. When I hopped into the Honda beside Duck, he didn't seem to notice there had even been any tears.

One, said the whisper.

I breathed it back and settled into the seat.

Duck rattled on the entire way, telling me how much he liked *The Crucible,* how he was sure Stevie was going to win the election tomorrow, and how he knew my voice was going to be okay.

"We've got the prom to look forward to," he said. "That's less than a week away. And Mrs. Isaacsen's hearing is tomorrow, too. You're gonna need a lot of support to get through that. It seems like your friends have all dumped you, but you've still got me—I'm there for you, and I mean it."

He punctuated it all with hand squeezes and hair touching and the look made from behind his sunglasses. I didn't do much at all, except say ONE over and over to myself. The right time was coming—the circles were moving closer together. I could almost see them.

When we pulled into the parking lot at the park, Duck took off his shades and searched my face as if he was looking for a missing person.

"I know you can't talk," he said. "So just shake your head or nod. Is anything wrong—I mean, besides all this stuff that's going on? Are you mad at me?"

One. No lying.

He reached out to touch the end of one of my braids, but I pushed his hand away and nodded.

"You ARE mad at me?" he said.

I nodded again.

Duck ran his palm over his head and darted his eyes all over my face. "Aw, man. No. Don't be mad at me, okay? I can't—"

And then before I even saw it coming, he was kissing me, both hands cupping my face, his lips begging at mine.

I wrapped my fingers around his wrists and pulled them away. I knew the panic in his eyes matched the freaked-out expression in my own. All I could do was grab my bag and haul myself out of the car. He called my name, but I just kept running, up and over the dunes with my legs fighting the sand, until I could lose myself in the crowd of cast and crew on the other side.

I didn't actually see individuals; I could just feel the familiarity, and I sank down into it, still clutching my bag.

"What are YOU doing here?" said an all-too-familiar voice. "I didn't see you in the play."

I looked up at Gigi and tried not to curl my lip back at her the way she was curling hers at me. There was nothing harder NOT to do at that point.

"You're such a freak show," she said. "Why are you staring at me like that?"

I pointed to my button, pinned haphazardly to my swimsuit top. She put her hand over her mouth.

"Sorry," she said. There was an actual giggle creeping up her throat. "I just think it's so—appropriate."

Then she just stood there, looking down at me before she swept the beach with dark-blue eyes that were almost violet. It gave me a chance to get a grip on my shaking. As I watched Gigi, it struck me like a random drive-by thought—she could be really pretty if she'd only lose the look that said the world around her smelled like a trash dump.

Maybe it does, I thought. *Maybe she's surrounded herself with so much garbage that even she can't stand it anymore.*

At the moment she seemed to be regarding the entire cast party guest list as dumpster material, although it looked like she was trying to find one piece of trash in particular.

Once she'd decided that I would do as the chosen litter of the moment, she settled her sneer back on me.

"I guess you won't be doing much preaching now, will you?" she said. "It's about time GOD told you to shut your big mouth. The rest of us have been trying to do that ever since you moved here."

"No—it's YOU who needs to shut up!"

I don't know which of us was more stunned as we both turned to stare at Eve. She was behind me, facing Gigi with her hands on her negligible hips, her almost-flat chest angrily rising and falling in lime green as she breathed.

"Move on, Eve," Gigi said.

"No. I have a right to be here."

"I said move on—if you know what's good for you."

Eve folded her arms across her chest as if she were going to fold, but she kept her eyes steady on Gigi.

"I KNOW what's good for me now," she said.

I was staring so intently at Eve, I almost missed the expressions that shuffled through Gigi's eyes like a deck of cards. For a second there was surprise, then disbelief, followed by unmistakable anger. But she drew a cool, bored-with-this look and played it with her chin pulled in.

"Whatever, little girl," she said.

Then, without looking at either one of us, she turned on a bare heel and walked toward the water, her bottom straining against the dental floss she used for a bathing suit. I started to turn to Eve with about a thousand questions in my eyes, but a male hand wrapped itself around my arm.

"Please, Duffy," Duck whispered in my ear. "Just let me talk to you—I promise I won't try anything."

I knew I had to. This was the time, and I knew there wasn't going to be a better one. He wanted to talk—and I wanted to make him tell the truth.

I nodded without looking at him, and I followed him back over the dunes to the jetty side. It was empty except for a mom and two preschoolers scooping up hermit crabs. I wished my life could still be that simple.

Duck spread a towel far away from their delighted laughter and sat on it, patting it for me to sit, too, but I sank to my knees in the sand in front of him. He closed his eyes and tightened his lips into a line. When he looked at me again, I had to force myself to hold his gaze. I knew the pain I was seeing could hold me back. I had to remind myself that he was a better actor than Matt Damon.

"I've been, like, racking my brain trying to figure out why you're mad at me," he said. "And I keep coming up with nothing. Can't you just say one sentence—no, you can't—don't do it—you can't mess up your voice—I know how much you wanna sing." He puffed air from his cheeks. "Look, I'll just ask you yes and no questions, okay?"

I nodded. *Just talk yourself into a corner,* I wanted to say to him. *I'm listening.*

"Okay," he said. "Am I, like, being too possessive?"

I shook my head.

"Am I not possessive enough? Is it because I went out of town that one weekend, and I didn't come to see the play opening night?"

I rolled my eyes.

"Okay—it's not that. What about—I don't go to church and stuff? I mean, I really want to talk to you about what I believe and what I can't yet—only we haven't had a chance—" He peered closely at me. "So—that's part of it but not all of it?"

I nodded, and Duck put his hand on top of his head and scrunched up his eyes. I could definitely relate to his frustration, but I kept thinking *One, One.* I sure hoped God was thinking it, too.

Duck sat there with his hands clasped to the back of his neck. "Okay—so it's gotta be something I don't even know about."

Oh, you know about it. You just don't know that I know about it.

He was studying my eyes. "What are you trying to say? Dang! I wish I knew you better so I could read your mind. I thought I was getting to know you pretty well, and that's why I wanted to talk to you about some stuff—only now that you're already ticked off at me, you'll probably hear, like, two words and dump me—"

His voice trailed off, and an awful realization formed in his eyes.

"No," he said. "You didn't find out—"

I didn't even have to nod. Duck shook his head slowly.

"You gotta listen to me, okay?" he said. "It's not like you think. I mean it WAS, but then I—"

This time he stopped abruptly, as if someone had slapped a hand across his mouth. I followed his gaze to the top of the dunes, and I saw that someone had. Gigi's silhouette was sharply cut out by the sun behind her.

Duck muttered something under his breath, and with a kick of sand he was off the towel, running toward her. Gigi turned, and her nonchalant outline disappeared beyond the hill. I watched as Duck followed after her at a dead run and then vanished, too.

So it was true. And he had still tried to convince me that it wasn't— until SHE appeared with whatever magic power she had over people.

Well, over some people, I thought. Eve stood up to her—that had been a shock, hearing her tell Gigi that SHE was the one who needed to shut up, not me. She hadn't even budged when Gigi told her to, "Move on, Eve."

Move on, EVE.

I got very still. Gigi had called her by name. A lowly freshman. How did she even KNOW Eve, someone so beneath her notice?

Sure, Gigi had blown her off—but not before I'd seen that she was shocked and then mad.

That wasn't just about having some underclassman overstep the royal boundaries, I thought. *Gigi's way beyond that.* It wasn't her MO to even respond to a person she didn't know or want to know.

She knew Eve.

Dear God. Dear God—no!

I snatched up my bag and took off toward the dunes with only one mission in mind.

When I literally ran into K.J. just on the other side, it knocked me over.

She got right down on the sand beside me, her face so close to mine I could smell chips. When I tried to get up, she put a hand in the middle of my chest and shoved me back.

"Listen to me, Duffy," she said through her teeth. "I found out something."

I nodded. Eve, for the moment, was forgotten.

"I was eavesdropping on Mr. H. and Mrs. I.," K.J. said. "He came over to the house this morning and they thought I was still asleep, but I could hear every word they said."

I motioned impatiently for her to go on.

"They didn't say her name, but they talked about the kid that accused Mrs. I. as 'she.' It's a girl. I know that only narrows it down to half the kids Mrs. I. has, but at least it's something." She sat up on her knees. "Can you do something with that, Duffy?"

Before I could even nod, she was standing up.

"You have to," she said. "Please."

I stood up with her and took hold of her arm.

"What?" she said.

I held my hand about five feet from the ground to indicate Eve.

"What are you talking about? Look—write it in the sand. I'm no good at sign language."

The child was a genius. I bent down and wrote EVE with my finger.

"Little stage crew chick?" she said. "I saw her leave with Gigi and some guy." Her eyes widened. "It was that guy you've been hanging around with! That little tramp didn't steal your man, did she?"

I shook my head. When K.J. walked away, I rubbed Eve's name out with my foot and then slid down to the jetty side of the dunes again. The mom and her kids were gone, and there was only me. One.

This doesn't feel so much like One, God, I thought. *Now I know—only I don't have any proof. The hearing is TOMORROW, and Gigi's got a whole team under her power. What am I supposed to do now?*

One.

I got that part!

One.

I plopped down just outside the reach of the tide and dug through my bag for my cell phone so I could call Dad and have him come get me, now that my ride and my reason for being there were both gone. My hand touched on something smooth and cool and unfamiliar. I pulled it out and stared at it.

It was a blue vial—only not the same one the Secret Admirer had already given to me. This one was bigger and filled to the top. Still clutching it, I dug with my other hand and came up with the parchment envelope I knew would be there.

The bridegroom is near.
You have all you need.
There is Oneness.
Come, be united with him.

As my eyes brushed the last line, I felt a warmth beside me, a hand held out for me to take. I didn't even have to look up to know it belonged to Ponytail Boy.

chaptereighteen

Neither of us said a word as I followed him to a white Jeep with its top down and climbed into the passenger seat. There was no question that I would go with him, though I did have a few OTHER inquiries I wanted to make.

But I didn't even have to ask. As we left the beach area and drove along a small road that entwined among empty campsites, the wind lifted his ponytail like streams of sunlight. On the way he answered my unspoken queries one by one.

"You're ready to become One with your bridegroom," he said. "And it isn't me."

I must have looked disappointed because he smiled with a tenderness I had never seen on a human face before.

"You will receive more in this marriage than I could ever give you," he said. "I'm only the bodyguard."

That actually didn't surprise me. He had always been there in times of crisis—even if he did seem to take his time about getting there, in my opinion.

"I was sent to protect you from the things that are not One," he said. "But I always had to wait until after you found the keys to unlock the secrets yourself."

I held up my wrist where the bracelet dangled its keys.

"She doesn't know about me," he said. "The ride to her union was in a different chariot altogether." He patted the Jeep's dashboard. "He thought you would like this one."

For a moment I watched the sandy dunes and the waving pampas grass fall behind us as we turned toward home. It was as if the Jeep were floating, wafting me toward a place I knew, but where I would never live in the same way again.

"The vehicles—the guides—are different for each person," Ponytail Boy said. "But the Way is the same. The only door to oneness is through him. You've found it—you have the keys, and now you will have a perfect union."

His eyes smiled at me, those eyes that looked into me. I knew right then what I had never been able to understand before. He was seeing the Laura Duffy I could be but couldn't quite grasp myself. Now I could almost hold her in my hands. Almost.

"It won't be a perfect union here on earth, in this lifetime," he said. "But he knows that you will come closer than most. That's why he wants to use you. That's why you've had to suffer so much pain in such a short time—that's how we learn the secrets and master them."

I closed my eyes. When I opened them, we were in my driveway. I didn't even wonder how we'd gotten there.

"There will be more pain," the man said. It didn't seem right now to think of him as Ponytail Boy. "But it will never stop you from living and breathing who you are meant to be. You are anointed."

He put his hand over mine, and I uncurled my fingers from the vial I hadn't realized I was still holding. He pulled off the small cork and tipped some of the oil onto his fingertip. I knew to close my eyes, knew to stay very still while he formed a tiny cross with it on my forehead.

I even knew the words before he breathed them into me. "In the name of the Father, and of the Son, and of the Holy Spirit."

And then he whispered, "I liked being known as Ponytail Boy. Please remember me that way."

When I opened my eyes, he was gone, and I was in my bed, blinking at the morning sunshine shafting through my blinds. I felt as if I had slept a silver sleep for days, and I knew what would happen when I opened my mouth and said, "One."

My voice was rich and strong and clear.

Of course, Mom burst into tears when I went to the kitchen and told her I could talk. Then she immediately told me to hush up until my appointment—which wasn't until one o'clock.

I tried not to freak out about what still needed to be done before Mrs. I.'s hearing. If they had to run a bunch of tests on me, I would be lucky to even get to the school district office by four. And even after what had happened with my precious Ponytail Boy, I knew I still needed to get to Eve and Duck, if I could, and get them to go forward with whatever they knew. It was probably a good thing that conversation wasn't going to take place at school, I decided, because there I would have to worry about Gigi showing up in the middle of it. She wasn't going to be stupid enough to make an appearance at the hearing, I was sure of that.

Finally, we got in to see the middle linebacker of a voice doctor. He shoved a scope down my throat and after a lot of grunting and hmm-mming, pulled it out and said, "I don't see what Dr. Sutherland described to me. They look like perfectly healthy vocal cords to me."

He was still shaking his head when he told me that if I even started to lose my voice again, I was to come see him immediately. As I thanked him, I was pretty sure I wouldn't need his services again.

"I have to go to Mrs. I.'s hearing, Mom," I told her on the way home. "I'm just going to go in the house and get my keys and go, or I won't make it in time."

Mom was still wiping at her eyes. "Promise me you won't overdo it with your voice. I know what that doctor said, but—"

"I'm going to try to get other people to do the talking," I said. I made a silent promise to myself to tell her and Dad everything tonight when it was over. There just wasn't time now.

Mom dropped me off and went on to pick up Bonnie at school. I went inside, and when I came out, there was somebody else parked in the driveway behind me. I actually had to rub my eyes to make myself believe it was the Expedition.

There were five bodies in the car, but only one got out. Celeste ran toward me, and I could read the "Have-I-got-something-to-tell-you!" message in the way she was flapping an envelope over her head.

"What's wrong?" I said.

Her eyes widened. "Your voice!" she said. And then she put the envelope in my hand. "Michelle has been looking for you all day. She said you HAD to have this right away."

The envelope was sealed and had a sticker on the flap, as if Michelle had wanted to make sure nobody else opened it. Celeste hadn't, but from the potty dance she was doing, it was obvious she was going to rip it open if I didn't do it in the next seven seconds.

There was a note inside from Michelle—

This is a list of the people Mrs. Isaacsen saw in her office the week before the accusation was made. I hope this helps you. Please don't let anyone else see this.

I looked up at Celeste, who was obviously trying to read the note from the other side. It was the closest I'd been to her in days, and I wanted to throw my arms around her and tell her everything. She would have welcomed it. I could see that in her eyes.

But I couldn't. Not yet. Michelle had taken a big risk, and she didn't need any trouble from it.

I folded the note back into the envelope and stuck it in my pocket. "Thanks," I said. "Are you going to the hearing?"

"Yeah." Her voice was all over the place with frustration. "They said no students can sit in on it, but we can at least be in the hall so Mrs. I. knows we're there."

"Okay," I said. "I'll see you there."

Celeste started to turn away, then turned back to me, then did the whole thing all over again. Finally, she said, "Do you want to ride with us?"

I drew in a big breath before I said, "Let me just make sure I have all my stuff out of my car—"

But I let the sentence drop when I saw a parchment envelope sitting on the front seat.

"I think I'd better drive myself," I said. We looked at each other for an agonizing moment, and then she said, stiffly, "Whatever."

It was all I could do not to run after the Expedition as it rolled out of the driveway, but as soon as it was gone, I scrambled into the car and tore open the Secret Admirer's note.

*The union of circles will take place
behind the school administration building.
The ceremony will begin promptly at 3:30.
Reception to follow.
Ponytail Boy*

There was too much spinning in my head for me to grab onto any of it except the time. I glanced frantically at the clock on the dashboard as I fired up the car. It was already 3:20, and I had at least ten minutes' worth of traffic to go through.

I squealed and honked and edged my way through it all like a whip was being cracked over my head. But once I pulled into the front parking lot of the Bay County School District building, the questions flooded in.

I'm supposed to go BEHIND the building?

But isn't the hearing inside?

Of course it is, genius. So why back there?

Is it safe?

Don't be a fool—this is Ponytail Boy guiding you.

I picked up the invitation. He had definitely signed it with his own name this time. He'd said there would be pain, but I would be protected.

"Okay," I said out loud. "Then let the union take place."

I could hear the voices before I even got to the back of the building. They were coming from the other side of the trash dumpster.

"You have to go through with it now—"

"I can't! It's a lie!"

"They'll want to know which is the lie—it happened, or it didn't happen. Either way you're busted."

"Then so are you!"

"You're on your own. You can't prove I had a thing to do with it."

I didn't even need a visual to know it was Gigi and Eve. But when I got to the other side of the dumpster, I saw Fielding holding Eve from behind as Gigi clawed her fingernails neatly down the girl's cheek. If Eve cried out, I didn't hear her over my own scream.

"Let her go! Let go of her!"

I got Eve by the arm and tried to pull her away, but Gigi was on me, locking my arms behind my back. All I could see was Eve in front of me, blood popping out in straight lines on her face, eyes on the cliff edge of hysteria. I forced my breathing to slow down. If I didn't stay calm, Eve was going to lose it.

"Eve," I said. "Listen to me."

"Oooh—she's had the miracle cure," Gigi said to Fielding. "She speaks!"

"Listen to me, Eve," I said. "It's going to be okay. We're protected."

Gigi snorted. "By who?"

"By us, Witch Woman, so look out!"

It was Celeste's husky voice slashing through the air in all directions. Stevie's was more commanding.

"Get off her, Gigi. Fielding—let go."

To my utter amazement they both did. But it wasn't because of

Celeste or Stevie. Nor was it due to K.J. and Joy Beth, who were brandishing baseball bats—or even Trent, who looked uncharacteristically formidable in his sunglasses and doubled-up fists.

It was obviously the sight of the two adults standing BEHIND the BFFs that made Fielding drop her hold on Eve and triggered Gigi to let go of me and bolt for the parking lot.

"Go after her, Trent!" Joy Beth said.

"Don't worry about it," Celeste said. She held up a wad of wires. "Her Mustang won't get very far without these."

The rest of the BFFs and K.J. made a circle around Fielding while Pastor Ennis strode across the lot after Gigi.

"Laura," Mr. Howitch said, "take Eve inside. They're going to be calling her in any minute. You all go with her. I've got this one handled."

Not that it would take much. Fielding was on the ground in a sobbing heap.

The BFFs and K.J. practically carried Eve and me into the building, talking over each other the whole way.

"We all got these invitations to your wedding, Duffy—"

"Talk about feeling like we were out of the loop!"

"We thought it was bogus—"

"We weren't even gonna come—"

"Who gets married behind the school admin building?"

"Who gets MARRIED?"

"K.J. told Mr. Howitch about hers—"

"And he said he got one, too—so that's why we all came—"

"Plus I saw yours in your car, Duffy, so I knew it was for real—"

"So we pull in here, and there's Pastor Ennis with his invitation in his hand—"

"You've got some explaining to do, girlfriend."

But there was no time for that. They set Eve and me down on a bench in the hall, right next to a closed door with a sign on it that said,

HEARING IN PROGRESS. DO NOT ENTER UNTIL CALLED.

Eve went limp against me.

"Get her some water, somebody," Stevie said.

Trent bolted for the water cooler.

"Stay with us, Evie," I said. "What do you have to do in there?"

Eve put a hand to her sliced-up cheek and started to cry.

"I told you Gigi was a witch!" Celeste said.

I suddenly thought of something and pulled Michelle's note out of my pocket. I ran my eyes down the page and stopped on the name I had hoped wouldn't be there—Eve Partlowe.

I pulled Eve toward me by both shoulders. "I know it was you, Eve. And I know who made you do it. But you have to tell."

"Tell what?" Celeste said.

"Later," K.J. said. She nudged me aside and got her face into Eve's. "Don't be like Mary Warren. Tell the truth, or you'll end up just like Gigi and her crowd."

"Whatever it is," Stevie said, "you have to do what's right, no matter what it costs you. I lost the election, but at least I know I played fair."

Joy Beth got next to Eve. She dwarfed her, but her voice was soft. "You gotta listen to Duffy. She once told me you do what you have to do—even when you're scared—because you've got God. It worked for me. You gotta listen to her."

Eve's eyes went from one of us to the other, all those faces encouraging her to do the right thing when most of them didn't even know what she was facing. My whole chest was swelling up.

"I want to," she said. "I tried to get away from Gigi and them—I really did. And I got to be your friend because I thought it would make me better—and then she found out about it, and she threatened me—"

"All right, look," Celeste said. "There's only one thing to do."

"Pray," Stevie said.

K.J. was the first one to stick out her hands for the holding. Joy Beth plunged right in.

"God—we're all a bunch of losers when it comes to havin' faith in you—all except Duffy. But we're comin' to you now, and we're bringin' Eve because she needs faith—she needs it big time—and she needs it right away."

"And if she can't find it yet," Celeste said, "then listen to our prayer because we do have faith—"

"Even if we forget that sometimes."

I almost cried when I heard Trent say that.

And then Stevie said, "And all God's people said—"

"Amen!"

"I'll 'amen' whatever they said, Lord," Pastor Ennis said with a grin as he came down the hall with Mr. Howitch and a cop who had Gigi firmly in tow. Her eyes were viciously riveted to the ground.

Behind us the door opened. Then it was my turn to go limp.

Duck stepped out, looking pasty and shaken. He jerked a little when he saw us, but his eyes went straight to Eve.

"I did my part," he said. "Now you do yours."

"Yes, EVE," Gigi said. Her words were like bullets. "Go in there and tell the truth."

"Not your version, Gigi," Duck said. "The real version."

"I will," Eve said. "But what if they don't believe me? I've already lied so much—"

"Don't let her take you down, Eve!" I said.

And then I stopped because I could feel Duck stepping up behind me.

"I told them what Gigi made you do," he said. "Now you have to go in there and back it up."

"YOU!" Gigi's yell reverberated off the ceiling, and suddenly Gigi was out of the grip of the policeman and on me with her fingernails flashing. Duck picked me up and hauled me out of the melee that ensued as Trent and the girls piled on top of her. It took Pastor Ennis, Mr. Howitch, and the police officer to peel them off so the cop could put handcuffs on her.

And yet she was still thrashing around, sneering and pointing her eyes at me like she'd just won.

"You see?" she snarled at me. "You see how many people it takes to protect you from me? Where was GOD, huh?"

From up in Duck's arms, I smiled a shaky smile down at my friends.

"He was right here, Gigi," I said. "You just saw him at work."

"Let's take her to Mr. Wylie," Mr. Howitch said to the cop. "He's waiting in the board room."

Gigi was still fighting with her handcuffs as the cop dragged her off. Pastor Ennis took Eve inside the hearing room.

"Heck of a way to get married, Duffy," Celeste said. She looked up at Duck, who was still holding me off the ground. "Did I miss something?"

"A lot," I said as I wriggled away from him. "But maybe we shouldn't talk about it here."

"Let 'em drag me right in there with Mrs. I.," Joy Beth said. "I shoulda stuck with Duffy in the first place."

She jabbed Trent, who nodded, not all that reluctantly.

"I wasn't the one who brought you all here just at the right time," I said. "I didn't send those invitations. That's a whole other story." I turned to Stevie. "You lost the election?"

She tipped her head toward the door where Gigi and the cop had just exited. "I don't think so now."

"That's right!" Celeste turned to high-five K.J., but K.J. turned and slid down the wall to sit on the floor.

We circled her, of course, and I took a chance and grabbed her hand. She clung to it like I was the last lifeboat.

"It's okay, K.J.," I said. "Mrs. I. is, like, ONE with God. No matter what happens, her integrity and all the good stuff we love about her will win."

"Is that gonna keep me out of a foster home?" K.J. said. "I can't go there. I can't."

"Not gonna happen."

We all looked at Duck. He was sitting outside the circle, apart from us.

"Like you know," K.J. said to him.

"I just saw those people's faces in there when I was talking. They believed me. I was stuttering all over the place, but they looked at me like they were taking every word I said like it was the gospel, and that's never happened to me before with adults." Duck loosened the tie I hadn't realized he was wearing and reached inside his shirt to pull out the cross medal. "It wasn't me—it was this."

"What is that, some kind of lucky charm?" Celeste said.

"No—I don't mean it was the medal—it just made me think of what Duffy says about believing. I figured I lost her, but I might still have a chance to be a freak." He looked at the floor. "Sometimes you don't know what you've got 'til it's gone—but I don't think God's gone. I think he'll make those people hear the truth from Eve."

The entire circle swiveled their heads to gaze at me.

"You let this guy go, Duffy?" Celeste said. "What were you thinking?"

My own gaze clinked with Duck's. We would be talking soon. There was a lot to sort out.

"Mrs. I.!"

K.J.'s announcement brought us all to our feet as Mrs. Isaacsen appeared through the door. But then we all just stood there, and nobody said anything. We didn't have to.

We could read it in the smile that broke across the face we loved so much.

"It looks like you're stuck with me," she said.

Everyone was on her in a joyful clatter of questions and answers and just plain squeals.

All except me.

I took a second to lean against the wall and close my eyes, listening for what I knew was waiting to be heard.

The whisper came.

One, it said.

I knew the circles had come together. Now my journey was to keep them there.

As I looked at the crazy, clawing crowd that was once again one with me, I knew I had a really good chance.

Book 1
RETAIL $6.99
ISBN 0310243998

Book 2
RETAIL $6.99
ISBN 031025180X

Book 3
RETAIL $6.99
ISBN 0310251826

A new series of fiction for teenage girls, the *'Nama Beach High* series is engaging and entertaining. Books 1-3 follow the life of Laura Duffy as she moves to a new school, gets a new job and a secret admirer. Follow Duffy on her adventures as she meets new friends, as well as God, and learns what it's like to adjust to a new place and a new faith.

invert

Visit www.invertbooks.com or your local bookstore.

How do you see yourself? How does God see you? Super models, positive thinking, self-help books, diets, cosmetics, dating guides--they are all supposed to make you more self-assured. But they often wind up leading to confusion, disappointment, and insecurity.

secret power
for girls
Identity, Security, and Self-Respect in Troubling Times
susie shellenberger

Secret Power for Girls hits the huge questions you have about yourself and about your image and gives you answers, help, and strength.

invert